ALL BECAUSE OF BAXTER

When Ellie's marriage unexpectedly ends, she and her young son Jacob seek refuge with Ellie's cousin Angie. But Angie soon tires of her house guests, including her own boisterous rescue dog, Baxter. When Baxter literally bumps into Dylan, Ellie dares to dream of a happy ending at last. But time is running out for them, and it seems Dylan has a secret that may jeopardise everything. Must Ellie give up on her dreams, or can Baxter save the day?

SHARON BOOTH

ALL BECAUSE OF BAXTER

Complete and Unabridged

LINFORD
Leicester

First published in Great Britain in 2015

First Linford Edition
published 2017

A catalogue record for this book is available
from the British Library.

ISBN 978–1–4448–3219–8

Published by
F. A. Thorpe (Publishing)
Anstey, Leicestershire

Set by Words & Graphics Ltd.
Anstey, Leicestershire
Printed and bound in Great Britain by
T. J. International Ltd., Padstow, Cornwall

This book is printed on acid-free paper

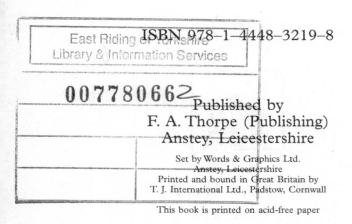

1

Another Waif and Stray

'Don't look like that! It'll be fun, having him around. Besides, Jacob will love him!'

Angie's face told a different tale. She was already having doubts, that much was obvious. Ellie stared at the Boxer dog, whose broad chest tensed as it strained on the lead, clearly desperate to be allowed to investigate this strange new world.

'Where on earth did you get it? And, more to the point, why?'

Angie had never struck Ellie as a dog lover before. Angie's mum wasn't one for animals — far too house proud — so Angie had never had any pets, even as a child. What could have possessed her to bring a dog into this already crowded house?

Angie sighed and collapsed onto the sofa — the warm cream, almost brand-new sofa. Ellie wondered how long it would look as pristine as it did at that moment. Not long, she suspected, looking at the Boxer dog's shiny red coat. She could well imagine both the sofa and their clothes coated in dog hair before long. How would Angie react to that?

'They didn't want him! Can you believe it? Poor little thing.'

Poor *little* thing! Ellie eyed the broad skull of the dog dubiously. 'Little' wasn't a word she'd use to describe him. All right, he wasn't of St Bernard proportions, but he was heavy-set, and certainly no lap dog. He stared back, big brown eyes looking mournfully at her out of a black face. He had a flash of white on his chest and some white on his legs, but the rest of him was a gorgeous reddish-brown colour. She had to admit, he was a handsome chap, in a battered prize-fighter sort of way.

'Who didn't want him?' Ellie asked her cousin.

'The owners. Well, there was this card, you see, in the shop window. He was being offered for free to a good home. I wasn't going to enquire at first, because I was sure plenty of people would want him, but then I got talking to Mrs Wilson who runs the shop and she told me all about it, and it was so *sad*.'

Ellie nodded, understanding the situation clearly now. The dog was another of Angie's lost causes. She couldn't resist a sob story, and would always step in to help if she could. Ellie could hardly complain. She was one of Angie's lost causes herself, and where would she and Jacob have been if not for her kind heart? The trouble was, Angie tended to jump in, letting her emotions rule her common sense, but quickly lost interest. Ellie had an uncomfortable feeling that time was already running out for her. Angie hadn't said anything outright, but there had been a distinct change in her attitude lately; a lot of mutterings about Jacob's toys, and how much the washing machine was getting used these days. She couldn't help but think that a dog would simply add to her cousin's stress.

'What did Mrs Wilson tell you about him?'

'The owner doesn't want him anymore because his new girlfriend doesn't like dogs. Can you believe it? They've been together for five years — the owner and the dog, I mean, not the owner and the girlfriend. *They've* probably only been together for five minutes. How shallow can you be? And poor Baxter here is out on his ear because of some stupid woman who's more than likely afraid of getting dog hairs on her best dress.'

Her lip curled in scorn and Ellie tried to hide a smile, wondering how Angie would react when her own clothes were covered in short red hairs. Still, she felt a sudden pang of sympathy for Baxter, and reached out a hand to stroke his silky ears. He immediately bounded forward, almost pulling Angie off the sofa and forcing her to drop the lead. Free from all restraint, he hurled himself at Ellie, planted his paws on her shoulders, and gave her a huge slobbery kiss.

'Ugh, get down!' She wiped her face,

her nose wrinkling in disgust. Baxter licked her again and she tried to push him away, but he nuzzled into her neck. She could hear him snuffling against her ear, and tried to quell her sudden panic. He was so heavy. He would knock Jacob over with no trouble at all.

'What if he's not safe? You don't know anything about him,' she whispered, wondering as she did so why she didn't want Baxter to hear. It wasn't as if he would understand, was it?

To her relief, Baxter released her and decided to wander round the living room, investigating the premises. As they watched him sniffing every inch of the carpet, Ellie repeated her worries. Jacob was just seven years old and no match for a dog of this size if it decided it wanted to play rough.

'Mrs Wilson's known Baxter for ages,' Angie said, 'and she said he's an angel with children, and really good-natured and affectionate. More than can be said for the owner's girlfriend. I took one look at her and decided he's better off out of it. She couldn't wait to get rid of him.'

'Didn't the owner seem sad to lose him?'

'He wasn't even there. Obviously couldn't be bothered to say goodbye. Poor boy.'

Ellie watched as Baxter stuck his head in the giant plant pot and sniffed the yucca that was Angie's pride and joy. She couldn't help sympathising with the dog. She knew only too well what it felt like to be dumped for a new model. Laura was only twenty-two — a full eight years younger than Ellie. She wondered what Tom was doing right now. Did he ever think about her? Did he regret what he'd done? Or was he still so entranced by his new girlfriend that his wife never even crossed his mind? *Ex-wife*, she reminded herself, her nails digging into her palms. The divorce was final now. No going back.

'Get off my yucca!' Angie jumped up and pulled a reluctant Baxter away, just as he'd stamped one foot in the plant pot.

'I hope he's house-trained,' said Ellie. 'That plant would make a great substitute for a lamp-post.'

'Oh no! You don't think he would?' Angie looked appalled. She cast a nervous glance around her immaculate living room.

Ellie grinned. 'I'm sure that at five years old, he's thoroughly house-trained. I was only teasing.'

Angie didn't look too sure.

'So where's his bed? His toys? Has she sent any food for him?'

Angie shook her head. 'She said his bed was old and shabby and she'd thrown it away, and I don't think it even occurred to her to send his toys. She was obviously a neat-freak. You know the type — blonde, glamorous, all made up. A real princess.'

Ellie bit her lip, trying not to smile as her blonde, glamorous, immaculately made-up cousin rambled on.

'I did get a bag of food for him, though. Well, half a bag. Although, come to think of it, she didn't give me any dishes for him ...'

Baxter gave a huge sigh and flopped onto the floor. Already there was a sprinkling of red hairs on the carpet.

'You'll have to get him a bed and dishes,' Ellie said. 'And some toys. Poor thing, not even a reminder from home to help him settle. Some people have no compassion.'

'Will you watch him for me while I nip out to the pet shop? I won't be long.'

'I have to collect Jacob from school.'

'No worries,' Angie said brightly. 'I'll collect him while I'm out and about.'

'But the school's in the opposite direction to the pet shop.'

'I'll take the car. I'll have plenty of time. Thanks a lot.'

There was no use arguing, and anyway, Ellie didn't feel able to. She owed her cousin, big-time. When Tom had broken the news that he'd fallen in love with Laura, it had left her in an impossible position.

Having decided that the only way they could afford to save for a decent deposit on a house of their own was to stop renting, Tom had approached his mother eighteen months previously to ask if he and Ellie and Jacob could stay at her house for a year or so while they saved. It had been a good plan from his point of view, although Ellie wasn't keen, having never really felt comfortable in his mother's forbidding presence.

When Tom moved in with Laura, Ellie had been desperate to get away, but it had proved difficult for her to find somewhere decent and affordable, and it turned out that Tom hadn't been saving for a deposit for quite some time — not since he'd fallen for the obvious charms of the lovely Laura, who, it seemed, had expensive tastes. If Angie hadn't offered her and Jacob a home, Ellie dreaded to think where they'd have ended up. And the most devastating thing about it was that Tom didn't appear to care a jot, airily telling her that she would be fine at his mother's and it would all sort itself out one way or another.

As the front door slammed, Baxter lifted his head and looked hopefully towards the hallway.

'Sorry, boy. That was just Angie going

out to get you some new things. Were you hoping to see your master?'

Baxter hauled himself up and padded over to her. He plonked his heavy head on her lap and gave another big sigh. In spite of her misgivings, Ellie felt a surge of compassion for the poor dog. She stroked his head between his ears and made soothing noises as he stood, silent and still, probably wondering where on earth he was and what was happening.

'I know how you feel, Baxter,' Ellie whispered, her eyes pricking with sudden tears. 'It's not easy being cast aside by someone you love, is it? At least you have us now, and you have a good home.'

But as for her and Jacob ... Ellie had no idea what was to become of them. She had an uneasy feeling that they would soon be leaving this house behind them, and where they would end up she dreaded to think.

* * *

As predicted, Jacob was thrilled to meet Baxter. Ellie watched, her heart in her mouth, as Baxter bounced over to greet her son when he arrived home from school, his face flushed with excitement.

'Angie says we've got a —' His words were cut off as Baxter leapt through the hallway door and skidded to a halt at his feet. 'Oh, wow! Isn't he gorgeous? Hello, boy. I'm Jacob. Who are you?'

'This is Baxter,' said Ellie, noting with relief that Baxter was being very careful around Jacob, although he was obviously delighted to meet him. It appeared Mrs Wilson had been right; he knew how to treat small children. One less thing to worry about, anyway.

Jacob was on his knees now, his arms around the dog's chest. Baxter emitted some very loud snuffly noises as he sniffed the boy's hair, neck, face, and school jumper. Whatever he discovered about him from these investigations obviously pleased him, as he rewarded Jacob with a huge lick across his cheek. Jacob giggled while Ellie winced.

'Okay, Jacob. That's enough for now. You'd better get changed or you're going to be covered in …' She sighed. Too late. As Jacob stood up she could see that the bright blue of his school jumper was now liberally dotted with red hairs. She'd have to put the washing machine on again, as his grey trousers were just as bad. This was going to be a nightmare.

'Where's Angie?' Ellie asked.

'Getting Baxter's things from the boot. She's got him loads of stuff, Mum. Is he really going to be living with us forever?'

Ellie felt a lump in her throat. 'Well, he's Angie's dog now, Jacob. Don't forget, we'll be moving out soon. We can't stay here much longer. It's not fair on Angie, is it?'

'Angie doesn't mind! Angie, you don't mind, do you?'

Angie pushed her way through the front door, staggering under the weight of a huge plastic dog bed which was packed with carrier bags full of pet shop purchases.

'Can you close the door for me, someone? Oh, my back's killing me. This stuff weighs a ton. Mind what, Jacob?'

'It doesn't matter,' said Ellie hastily, shutting the front door and removing some of the bags from the dog bed. 'Jacob, take Baxter back into the living room and then go upstairs and change. I'll have to wash your uniform for tomorrow.'

'You wouldn't mind if me and Mum stayed here with you, would you?' Jacob pleaded with Angie. 'Mum says we have to move out, but it's nice here, and now you've got Baxter it'll be even more fun.'

Ellie daren't look at Angie and headed straight to the kitchen instead. Behind her she heard Angie muttering, 'Well, thing is, Jacob, your mum needs her own place. Wouldn't you like it to be just you and her? Your own things around you again? Your own home?'

Ellie heard Jacob's reply and dropped the carrier bags onto the worktop, feeling sick: 'Not really a home without Dad, though, is it? He won't come back, will he? It wouldn't be the same.'

Ellie closed her eyes, trying desperately to hold back the tears. There it was again, that fierce stab of guilt. Why was she the one feeling guilty when it was Tom who'd lied and cheated? Tom who'd walked away and left them behind with, it seemed, hardly a second thought. She'd wondered so often over the last few months if she'd ever really known him at all. Had the young man she'd married nine years ago really been the sort of person who'd be capable of such cruel disregard for his wife and child?

Yet, as she thought back over their relationship, she'd had to acknowledge that the signs had been there from the very beginning. Everything had been the way he wanted it: when and where they were married, where they lived, when they started a family, the fact that there was only ever going to be one child ... She wondered, not for the first time, why she'd gone along with his wishes so easily. What had happened to her? How had he managed to chip away at her self-esteem so easily? Why had she accepted life on his terms?

Well, it was done now. He'd done her a favour, moving in with Laura. Now she had the chance to start doing the things that she wanted to do. The question was, what exactly *did* she want?

The answer came to her with sickening clarity. A decent home for herself and Jacob, more children, someone who loved her unconditionally. Someone who would never lie or cheat. Someone who would love Jacob as his own.

She shook her head and began to unpack the bags as Angie dumped the dog bed on the kitchen table. There was no point even thinking such things. The future was Jacob, and somehow she had to find a decent home for him. The problem was, how? She'd asked for more hours at work, but they were fully staffed, and she'd applied for so many full-time jobs she'd lost count. On her wages from the supermarket, the best she would be able to afford was some dingy flat somewhere in town. It didn't bear thinking about. What kind of life would that be for her precious son?

'I had no idea dogs needed so much stuff!' Angie reached over and picked up a

15

carrier bag, rummaging around inside it. 'Look at this. Dog toothpaste and a dog toothbrush. Who knew? How the heck am I supposed to clean his teeth?'

'Rather you than me,' said Ellie. 'I think they've sold you half the shop.'

'He said they were just the basics, but to be honest I'm not so sure. This lead cost me a fortune.'

'But he already has a lead!'

'I know. But when I described it to the man in the shop he said it was the wrong sort of lead and sold me this one instead.'

She looked quite puzzled and, in spite of her gloom, Ellie couldn't help laughing. 'He saw you coming. I should have gone with you. I'd have stuck to the essentials.'

'And since when were you so assertive?' demanded Angie. 'What happened to the girl who wouldn't say boo to a goose?'

'She grew up,' sighed Ellie. 'She had to, pretty fast.'

Angie put her arm around her. 'I'll make us a cup of tea, then we'll sort all this stuff out properly. Did you say you were washing Jacob's school uniform?'

'Yes, sorry. Dog hair. I've bought some washing powder.'

'It's okay, but while you're washing his stuff, you couldn't shove this top in, too, could you? I look like the Yeti with all this hair on me.'

Ellie gave her a wry look. 'Looks like we're going to be doing quite a lot of washing and vacuuming now that you've got Baxter.'

'I know.' Angie looked pensive for a moment, then she brightened. 'But he's so lovely, isn't he? He deserves a second chance. It'll all be worth it in the end.'

Ellie headed back into the living room to coax Jacob away from Baxter and persuade him to change his clothes, but not before she'd noticed Angie cross her fingers. She had a feeling that her cousin was already wondering what she'd let herself in for, and she wasn't the only one.

2

In the Dog House

'I'm going to kill that dog!' Angie's face was purple with rage as she waved her handbag in the air. 'Look what he's done now!'

'What's wrong?' Ellie paused in her dusting and noticed Baxter looking very guilty as he lurked in a corner of the room.

'What do you think's wrong? Look at my bag! He's chewed through the handles. My Prada bag, ruined!'

'Wasn't genuine Prada, was it? Stop winding yourself up.' Wayne, Angie's boyfriend, managed to drag his eyes away from the football match on the television long enough to utter an opinion.

'It may not have been genuine, but it still cost me over a hundred pounds. That wretched dog is driving me insane. Look at his face! He knows he's done wrong, but it won't stop him doing it again, will it?'

'I said you were crazy to get a dog. What did you want one for, anyway? They're nothing but trouble. You and your lost causes. You're too soft by half and you always end up regretting it,' Wayne said, casting a sly look at Ellie.

She turned away, refusing to give him the satisfaction of seeing how much his words hurt. Since he'd been on the scene, Angie had made it even more obvious that she would like to have her house back to herself. Ellie and Jacob were in the way, there was no doubt about it. There was only one thing for it: she would have to throw herself on Tom's mercy. The thought made her nauseous, but she was only just managing to pay the rent and her share of the bills and food to Angie. There was barely anything left over to save, and her deposit fund was still pitiful. Tom must have put some money away, surely? He earned plenty as a taxi driver, although being self-employed, he'd managed to convince the authorities that he was barely covering expenses and had been allowed to pay a nominal sum in child support. It was sickening. Maybe she could threaten to expose him? Blackmail was an ugly word, but so was 'slum', and she had no intention of subjecting Jacob to a life in some rundown flat somewhere.

'He's probably just bored,' Ellie said. 'Have you been taking him for regular walks?'

Angie plonked herself down beside Wayne and folded her arms. 'Yes, of course I have. He's just naturally naughty. I'm beginning to see why they wanted rid of him now. Bet it had nothing to do with the girlfriend. I think I've been had.'

'What do you expect when he was free to a good home?' demanded Wayne. 'Always dodgy, that. Look at him. He's a pedigree Boxer dog. They're worth good money. Why would they give him away when they could sell him? Had to be something wrong with him, and there's your answer. He's unmanageable.'

'Unmanageable?' Ellie shook her head and began dusting the television, just to annoy Wayne. 'He's hardly that. He's good most of the time. It's like I said; he's probably bored.'

'Do you mind? United have a penalty! Go and dust somewhere else.'

'It's all right for you, Ellie,' said Angie. 'You don't have expensive things, but Baxter's destroyed my best shoes and that pink cashmere jumper that I loved, as well as my bag. He's becoming a liability.'

Wayne grunted. 'You ought to get rid of him. Anything that's a liability should go. I've been telling you that for ages.'

He glared at Ellie and she marched into the kitchen, slamming the door behind her. For a moment she leaned against the sink, her heart pounding as she tried to quell the rage. Then she put the polish and duster away and headed upstairs.

Jacob was in his room watching television. It was Saturday, and Saturdays meant Wayne slobbing out on the sofa for the whole day, with the remote control welded to his hand. Jacob shared Ellie's opinion of Wayne and tended to keep out of the way.

Ellie leaned against the door frame, watching him as he concentrated on *Thunderbirds*. Her heart swelled with love and pride as she watched his beautiful little face, his big blue eyes wide with wonder at the adventures unfolding on the screen before him. She wondered how it was possible to love someone so much when he was the image of the man who'd hurt them both so badly.

'Has it nearly finished?' she asked him.

He looked up at her and nodded. 'Nearly. Can I have Thunderbird Three for my birthday, Mum?'

She smiled. 'Well, your birthday's a long way off yet, but we'll see. When it ends, do you want to come out with me? I think we should take Baxter for a walk; get him away from Wayne and Angie for a bit.'

He beamed at her. 'Yes, please.'

'Okay. I've just got to make a phone call. Finish with your programme and then we'll get ready.'

She headed into her bedroom and rummaged in her bag for her mobile phone. Sitting on the bed, she scrolled through the list of entries in her contacts and then paused, her finger hovering over Tom's name. Her stomach churned at the thought of speaking to him, but she had no choice. This was for Jacob, she reminded herself. Taking a deep breath, she pressed the call button and waited, her heart pounding, half hoping he wouldn't answer.

'Hello?'

'It's me, Ellie.'

'Yeah, I can read. What's up? Is Jacob all right?'

Well, that was a pleasant start to the conversation. Ellie pulled at the green cotton duvet nervously. 'It depends what you mean by all right, I suppose.'

'Look, Ellie, if this is another call to try to make me feel guilty and beg me to come home, forget it. We're done. I'm with Laura now. Deal with it.'

Ellie forgot all about her nerves as a wave of anger swept over her. Who the hell did he think he was? 'Come home? Come home to where? In case you'd forgotten, we haven't got a home any more, thanks to you and your bright ideas, not to mention your failure to save any money, in spite of all your promises.'

'Look, I've not got time for this. Laura's waiting for me. We're going into town. Is there a point to this conversation?'

'I need some money.' There, she'd said it. Was that to the point enough for him?

'Don't we all? What do you need it for?'

'I need a deposit for a flat or a house somewhere. I can't save much on my wages, and you owe me. You owe Jacob. The least you can do is make sure he has a decent roof over his head.'

'What's wrong with Angie's place?'

'She has a boyfriend now. She wants some privacy. You know as well as I do that this was only ever supposed to be temporary.'

'You should never have left my mother's. You were all right there. It's your own fault for being so stubborn.'

'My fault?' Ellie felt sick with anger.

The injustice was almost too much to bear. 'Look, I'm not going to argue all day about this. Can you lend me some money for a deposit or not?'

'Not.'

'Are you joking? You must be able to lend me something.'

'Is that Ellie?' Ellie's stomach did a huge somersault as she heard Laura's voice in the background. 'What's she moaning about now?'

'Look, Ellie, I've got to go.'

'You can't go yet. I need some help. I can't stay here much longer and we have nowhere to go. I know you don't care about me, but you have a son here who needs a decent home.'

'Tell her we're going out,' demanded Laura. 'Come on, babes, it's nearly two o'clock now.'

'Ellie, I have to go. I haven't got any money. I'm completely broke. I'd lend you some if I had any, but I haven't.'

'Is she after money?' Laura sounded outraged. 'Of all the nerve. She's working, isn't she? Tell her to tighten the purse strings. We've got enough to pay for. Weddings don't come cheap.'

'Weddings?' Ellie's throat tightened. 'Did she just say weddings? Are you getting married?'

'Yeah, yeah. I was going to tell you. So you see, I really don't have any cash to spare. Have you thought of asking the council? They might give you a flat somewhere.'

'There's a waiting list a mile long, and besides, you know what their flats are like. I can't —'

'Babes, will you hurry up? We've got a wedding fair to get to!'

'Coming, honey. Sorry, Ellie. Got to go, really. Get yourself to the council. They'll sort you out. Tell Jakey I'll see him next Sunday. Bye.'

The phone went dead. Ellie stared at the screen as it switched back to a picture of Jacob, smiling up at her with innocent eyes. So that was the answer — throw herself on the mercy of the council and pray that, if she were very lucky, they'd give her one of the empty high-rise flats on one of the town's estates? She knew what they were like. She couldn't have stood living there herself, never mind expecting her son to. What now?

Numbly, she pulled on her trainers and found her jacket. So Tom and Laura were getting married. That hadn't taken them long. Amazing that he could find the money to pay for a wedding, but couldn't spare anything to put a roof over his child's head.

She felt a sudden bitterness and tried hard to let it go. It wouldn't help. If it could provide a home for herself and her son she would have wallowed in it all day, but the cold fact was that no amount of bitterness or pain or anger would change the situation. She had to move on and she also had to face facts. She wasn't going to get any help from anyone. She would have to sort things out for herself, and she would. She'd find a decent home for them, if it meant scouring every news-paper, every online property site ... If it meant moving away.

She paused. Would she move away?

This was the town where she'd grown up. It was all she knew. Could she really bring herself to leave? But then, what was there for her now? She had no family of her own left here, apart from Angie, since her mother had moved to Spain after her father died. And she could always make new friends. Maybe she could find a job that paid higher wages somewhere else. If it could give them a better life, it would be worth the upheaval.

Feeling a new determination, she headed back into Jacob's room and was pleased to see him fastening his jacket. '*Thunderbirds* finished?'

He nodded. 'It was F-A-B. Where are we going?'

She shrugged and held out her hand for his. 'I'm not sure. The park? The woods? We'll see where our legs carry us, eh?'

He laughed and squeezed her hand and together they went downstairs. Wayne and Angie looked at them as they entered the living room.

'Going out?' Angie barely tried to keep

the delight from her voice.

'Thought we'd take Baxter for a walk,' Ellie said. 'He's obviously bored, and Jacob could do with some fresh air. You don't mind, do you?'

'Feel free,' said Angie. 'You know where his lead is.'

'Yeah, and take your time,' said Wayne. 'No need to rush back.'

He and Angie grinned at each other, and Ellie ushered Jacob into the kitchen, calling for Baxter as she did so. He appeared immediately, his whole demeanour changing as he recognised the fact that he was about to get out of the house.

'I don't blame you, Baxter,' whispered Ellie as she clipped the lead to his collar. 'I can't wait to get out of here, too. Looks like we've both outstayed our welcome.'

3

A Walk in the Park

Baxter pulled hard on his lead. It took all Ellie's strength to restrain him, and she was out of breath by the time they reached the park.

'He's glad to be outside, isn't he, Mum?' said Jacob, laughing as Baxter snorted, apparently in full agreement.

'He certainly seems to be,' said Ellie. She wondered exactly how much exercise the dog had been getting. Angie was a proofreader, working from home, and she had assured Ellie that she was taking him for regular walks, but Ellie wasn't so sure. She'd certainly made no attempt to walk him today. Was she being economical with the truth? Maybe that was why Baxter was being so naughty. He probably had loads of energy that just wasn't getting used up.

'Are we going to feed the ducks?' Jacob scanned the lake ahead of them. He loved the ducks. There was a small hut at the side of the lake which sold duck food, and they'd come here regularly since he was a toddler in his buggy to throw the mixture of rice, corn and other grains that the park provided. The feeding of the ducks was strictly monitored. You could only feed them food bought at the park, and when that ran out there would be no more available that day. It seemed a sensible policy, and the food was cheap enough. It was worth every penny, anyway. Jacob had always gained so much pleasure from the activity.

'Let's see if they have any food left,' said Ellie. She wondered uneasily what Baxter would make of the birds and automatically tightened her hold on the lead. But though he sniffed the air curiously, he seemed unfazed by their presence, and as Jacob scattered the feed for them, he stood watching, quite amiably.

She thought again about the phone call. So Tom was getting married again.

How did that make her feel? Wretched, worthless, easily replaced. Yet, did it really matter? So he was marrying Laura. He was already living with her, so what difference did a piece of paper and a ring make? It wasn't as if being married had made much difference to Tom's loyalty to her, now, was it? Why should Laura be able to trust him any more than Ellie had? And she hadn't — not really. There had always been a nagging voice whispering a warning in her ear, right from the moment she'd met him.

He'd been so charming and attentive, but from the beginning, there had been something about him that made her uneasy. She'd always put her faith in her instincts until then, listening to that little voice that seemed to know whether someone could be trusted or not. It had whispered to her, from the first, that he was one of those people who kept secrets. He was sly. She'd caught him out in his lies many, many times, yet he always seemed to have an explanation, and a way about him that made her laugh it off and forgive him. The good times had been good, and had helped him fool her, but those times grew fewer and further between. Ellie had to be honest with herself. The relationship had stopped being a rewarding one many years ago. She was better off out of it. She wondered why that knowledge didn't fully take away the pain. Sometimes she wished she'd never met Tom Jackson.

Jacob giggled and threw the last of the food to the eager ducks. Baxter sat quietly beside them, watching these strange little creatures scrabbling for food, with keen interest. Jacob put the empty bag in his pocket and threw his arms around the dog.

'Good boy. He was very good, wasn't he, Mum? He wasn't naughty to the ducks, was he?'

Ellie smiled down at him. He was so beautiful. How could she regret meeting Tom, however things had turned out, when he'd given her this wonderful child? She ruffled Jacob's dark hair and nodded.

'He was very good. Shall we let him have a run around as a reward?'

Jacob clapped his hands. 'I'll race him. Can I race him, Mum?'

'Okay. Let's get away from the lake first, shall we? We'll go over to the field. Come on.'

They headed over to the far end of the park, Baxter pulling eagerly on his lead as if he sensed freedom was only moments away.

'Next time we should bring the Frisbee, shouldn't we, Mum? Or a ball? Shall we do that next time?'

'I think that'd be fun. I'm sure Baxter would like a game with you,' confirmed Ellie. She reached down and unclipped Baxter's lead. 'Okay, boy, off you go. Quick run around, burn off some of that excess energy.'

Jacob whooped with delight as Baxter leapt forward. 'Race you, Baxter!' he yelled, running after the dog, his arms waving with excitement. Baxter slowed, almost as if he was waiting for him to catch up, then they ran together across the field. Ellie walked in their wake, laughing at their joyful exertions. It was good to see Jacob letting off steam. He'd had a rough time of it lately, and he never complained. He'd really taken to Baxter, that much was obvious. She frowned, chewing her lip as she thought about the future. She would go online when she got home. Check out the flats and houses for rent again. Cast her net a bit wider. Jacob was going to have a decent home, no matter what the cost.

They were running back towards her now and she stood still, waiting. Jacob's face was flushed and his eyes were bright with laughter. Baxter could easily have outrun him, but he kept pace with the little boy, turning his head every now and then to check that Jacob was still with him. If Ellie hadn't known better, she'd have sworn the dog was smiling.

She threw open her arms and Jacob ran into them. 'I won! I won, didn't I?'

'I think you did,' she said, then looked round in alarm. 'Baxter! Baxter, come here!'

Baxter, having allowed Jacob to win the race, had apparently decided that was enough good behaviour for one day and had charged past her, streaking across the field with astonishing speed, weaving between children playing football and ignoring a couple of other dogs who wanted him to stop and play. Ellie grabbed Jacob's hand and they ran after him. She prayed silently that he wouldn't cause any trouble or head out of the park. She hoped he'd forgotten about the ducks.

He was almost at the other end of the field, where a man was busy texting on his mobile phone. He was wearing loose jogging pants and a sweatshirt, and was evidently concentrating on his phone so much that he was totally oblivious to the missile that was heading his way. Ellie watched in horror as the man, having shoved his phone back in his pocket, crouched down suddenly, fumbling with his trainers. Baxter cannoned into him, and Ellie yelped as the man fell flat on his back.

'Oh no! Oh, God, Baxter, what have you done?'

By the time Ellie and Jacob reached them, Baxter was licking the man's face as he lay, seemingly winded, on the ground.

'I can't apologise enough,' Ellie panted. 'He gets a little overexcited. It's the first time I've let him off the lead, and I think he was on an adrenaline high because he'd just been racing Jacob here. I don't think he meant to knock you over, but then you bent down, you see, and he wouldn't have been able to stop, and ... I'm so sorry.'

She peered down at the man, trying to decide if he looked angry enough to threaten to sue her. He blinked up at her, his face red, and she held her breath as he opened his mouth to reply. Baxter leaned over him and slurped his tongue all over the man's face. Ellie cringed, horrified. 'Baxter! Stop it, now!'

Baxter looked at her as if she were mad, but Jacob ran to him and grabbed his collar, pulling him, with great difficulty, away from the poor man, who was now rubbing his face, looking quite stunned.

'Ugh.'

Well, at least he could speak. That was something. Ellie had feared Baxter had knocked all the air out of his lungs. If he decided to make a fuss about it, Angie and Wayne would be furious. Baxter would be in even more bother and, of course, they would blame her. She couldn't afford a lawsuit.

'I'm so, so sorry.' She held out her hand to him and, after a moment's hesitation, he took it and allowed her to pull him to his feet. 'It's not his fault. He's had a tough time of it lately. He was abandoned by a cruel, heartless owner and he's still trying to settle in. I know he didn't mean to hurt you. Are you all right?'

'Well, I've been better,' he admitted. He surveyed Baxter, who wagged his tail furiously. 'Sounds like he's had a rough deal.' He sounded a bit shaky. Ellie hoped he wasn't concussed.

'Oh, he has. He just needs to settle, that's all. He's not a bad dog at all, just overexcited. He has a lot of energy and doesn't get to burn it off as much as he should.'

'Don't you take him for regular walks?'

'Well, he's not actually my dog.' Ellie didn't quite know how to explain the situation and her voice trailed off. The man rubbed the back of his neck. He was younger than she'd realised, probably in his early thirties, and had a shock of brown hair and grey-green eyes. The baggy sweatshirt and jogging pants didn't do him any favours. 'Were you going for a run? I'm sorry we interrupted you.'

He shook his head. 'Oh no, no. That's okay. I'm all done for today. I'm Dylan, by the way.'

He held out his hand and she took it, glad that he was being civil, and not threatening to call the police about her mad, uncontrollable dog. 'I'm Ellie, and this is my son, Jacob. And this, as you probably heard, is Baxter.'

Dylan smiled at Jacob, then reached over and patted Baxter, who immediately took a leap forward, nearly pulling Jacob over. Ellie grabbed him and clipped his lead back on.

'Baxter the Boxer, eh? Catchy.' He bent

down and made a huge fuss of the dog, which was pretty big of him in Ellie's opinion, given the circumstances. 'You're a beauty, aren't you? Aren't you a handsome boy? Yes, you are. Yes, you are.'

Baxter seemed thoroughly delighted with Dylan's opinion and made some very appreciative noises, while enjoying having his ears rubbed and his nose kissed.

'It's very good of you to be so understanding. Not many people would be.'

'I love dogs,' admitted Dylan. 'He didn't mean to knock me over. And if he's had a bad time of it ... Did you say he's not your dog?'

Ellie sighed. 'Sadly not. He belongs to my cousin. We live with her, you see, at least at the moment. She has a habit of taking in waifs and strays.'

The man raised an eyebrow and she hurried on, wondering why on earth she'd said such a thing. 'Poor Baxter here had been abandoned, and —'

'Abandoned?' Dylan's voice was sharp. 'What do you mean, abandoned? You mean he was a stray?'

'Well no, not exactly. He was free to a good home, but to be honest I don't think the 'good home' bit mattered at all.'

'Oh? Why not?' He stroked Baxter's head again and then turned back to Ellie. 'You think they'd have let just anyone have him?'

'They did,' she said grimly. 'Don't get me wrong, my cousin's lovely, but they didn't know that, did they? They didn't check out our home or anything. If they'd made even the most basic enquiries they'd have known that Angie's never owned a dog in her life, and this was more about her feeling sorry for Baxter and acting on a whim than actually wanting to bring a dog into her life.'

'I can't believe it.' Dylan shook his head.

'I know. They didn't even send any of his things with him. Apparently this Melissa woman had thrown everything away and Angie had to go out and buy everything from scratch.'

'So he had nothing from his old home?

Not even his bed? What about toys? Surely —'

'Nothing. The owner said they were dirty. Well, she wasn't actually the owner, she was his girlfriend, and Angie said she was horrible — a real princess type — but the owner is even worse in my opinion. He dumped the poor dog after five years because the girlfriend didn't like dogs. I mean, really! People like him don't deserve dogs. Don't you agree?'

'I do agree. The man's an idiot. I hope he feels racked with guilt and misses Baxter every single day,' said Dylan with some feeling.

'Poor Baxter couldn't settle, and of course he didn't even have anything with the scent of home on it to help him. Between you and me,' Ellie whispered, seeing that Jacob was now preoccupied with teaching Baxter to give him his paw, 'he wouldn't sleep on the new bed, and I found him lying on my cousin's best jumper, so I've been letting him sleep in my bedroom. Angie would kill me if she knew, but bless him, he needs company.'

'That's very good of you.' Dylan gazed into her eyes and smiled. He had a nice smile. Ellie found herself blushing. 'Baxter's very lucky to have you. Dogs like him need lots of time and attention to stop them getting bored. He'll be quite destructive if he doesn't get the love and exercise he needs.'

'You're obviously a dog lover,' said Ellie.

He nodded. 'Definitely. I come to this park a lot to walk my dog. We love it here. He sits with me as I feed the ducks, and he has a good run on this field, and sometimes we go to the woods, too. Although I've got to watch him there. Daren't let him off the lead, because if he scents a rabbit he's off.' He laughed, and his hand reached out for Baxter's head again.

'We've just fed the ducks, haven't we, Mum?' said Jacob. 'And Baxter was really good, too. What's your dog called?' he asked.

Dylan smiled. 'My dog? He's called Tyson.'

'Tyson? Is he another Boxer?' Ellie laughed.

43

'Why isn't he with you?' enquired Jacob.

'Well, I'm jogging.' Dylan shrugged.

'Doesn't matter. Tyson could jog with you,' said Jacob. 'Baxter ran with me. I beat him, though,' he confided.

Dylan laughed. 'Wow! You must run very fast, then. When I'm jogging, I like to concentrate. I take my running very seriously, young man. Tyson needs my full attention, so it wouldn't be fair on either of us.'

'Would you like to join us tomorrow?' Ellie wondered what on earth she was thinking, blurting that out. He'd think she was mad, and perhaps she was. It wasn't like her to ask a total stranger on a date. What was she talking about? It wasn't a date. She just wanted company — for Baxter.

Dylan was looking at her steadily, saying nothing. She wilted under the gaze from those soft grey-green eyes.

'Sorry. You're not likely to want to join us, are you? Not after Baxter's behaviour.' Yeah, put the blame on Baxter. Never mind her own odd behaviour.

He smiled suddenly. 'I think that'd be fun. It does get a bit boring walking Tyson alone every day, and it'd be good for Baxter to socialise with other dogs. What time?'

Ellie shrugged. 'It's Sunday. Any time would be fine by me.'

He considered. 'I can't get away too early tomorrow. Would eleven be all right? Normally it'd be earlier, but weekends are tricky.'

'Eleven would be perfect.' She found she was beaming at him and tried to straighten her face. He would think she was a complete lunatic at this rate. Perhaps she was. Perhaps the shock of Tom's impending marriage, her perilous living arrangements, and her worries about her financial situation were taking their toll on her nerves. Dylan was grinning at her, and she felt herself relax.

'Tomorrow at eleven. It's a date,' he said. 'See you tomorrow, boy,' he added, giving Baxter one last pat. 'And you, too, Jacob. Very nice to meet you,' he said, shaking the little boy's hand.

Jacob looked very pleased to be treated in such a grown-up fashion. 'Bye, Dylan. See you tomorrow.'

Dylan turned and began to jog slowly away from them. Baxter tried to follow but Ellie pulled him back with some effort. 'Oh no you don't! That's quite enough from you for today, thank you very much.' They watched Dylan running through the park gates, then Ellie turned back to Jacob. 'Right, well now all that excitement's over, let's get Baxter home, shall we?'

Jacob wrinkled his nose. 'S'ppose so. Will Wayne still be there?'

'Probably. You don't like him much, do you?'

'Not really. Can I go upstairs and watch telly?'

Ellie hesitated. 'Tell you what, how about we drop Baxter back home and then go into town? We could price up those *Thunderbird* toys at the toy shop.'

'Really? And can we have a milkshake at the burger bar?'

Ellie grinned and ruffled his hair. 'Why

not?'

'Hear that, Baxter? I'm going into town with Mum. It's a shame Baxter can't come with us, isn't it?'

'Hmm.' Frankly, Ellie thought a break from Baxter would be quite welcome. She'd had quite enough of his escapades that afternoon. Then again, if he hadn't had a rush of energy, she would never have met Dylan, and he seemed a nice, friendly sort of man. There were so many difficulties in her life at the moment, it would be a pleasure to be around someone so completely uncomplicated.

4

The Tortoise and the Hare

'You've been letting Baxter sleep in your bedroom, haven't you?' Angie's tone was accusing, and Ellie knew there was little point in trying to deny it.

'He wouldn't settle downstairs. He was crying. I felt sorry for him, and he's been no trouble at all'

'Huh! Apart from all the dog hairs on the bedroom carpet. That was new last year, you know.'

'They'll soon clean up. I'll run the vacuum cleaner over them in a minute.' Ellie frowned. 'What were you doing in my bedroom?'

Angie scowled. 'Er, I think you'll find it's my bedroom, actually. I was just checking the boiler, that's all.'

Ellie raised an eyebrow. 'Really? Why?'

'It was making a funny noise. Anyway,

48

that's not the point. I don't want that dog upstairs. It's my house and those are my rules.'

Ellie nodded. 'Fair enough. It won't happen again.'

'Good.' Angie flounced out of the room, but not before Ellie caught the scent of her own perfume. She'd had a feeling Angie had borrowed it before, as the bottle was emptying surprisingly quickly and Ellie hadn't worn it for a while. But there was no point confronting Angie about it. She would only deny it, and it would cause yet another scene; there'd been more than enough of those lately.

Ellie closed her laptop with a sigh. There was nothing affordable on the property sites she'd been checking out for the last hour, and all she'd achieved was to make herself feel even more dispirited. Time to cheer herself up. She glanced at her watch. She just had time to vacuum the bedroom carpet, and then she and Jacob could get Baxter's lead and escape to the park.

She frowned, realising that the situation really had sunk to an all-time low if she considered getting out of the house an escape. How had things got so bad? She and Angie used to be very close, even as children. Sharing a house for the last six months had taken its toll on their friendship, and she felt sad about that. Having Wayne around, making his sarcastic comments and urging Angie to get rid of her unwanted guests, wasn't helping the situation. Maybe she would have to approach the council after all.

She collected the vacuum cleaner from the cupboard under the stairs and dragged it up to her bedroom, pausing before she plugged it in to warn Jacob that they would be leaving very soon, and he'd better get his shoes and jacket on.

He was ready before she'd even finished vacuuming, obviously as keen as she was to get out of the house. Baxter, who had been curled up under the kitchen table, looking extremely sorry for himself, nearly knocked a chair over in his eagerness when he saw them approaching, his lead dangling from Ellie's hand.

'Come on then, and no misbehaving today,' Ellie warned as she opened the back door and they set off for the park.

'Do you think he'll be all right with Tyson?' asked Jacob. 'Some dogs don't like other dogs, do they?'

'He didn't bother with those loose dogs that wanted to play yesterday, did he?' Ellie reassured him. 'And he was good with the ducks, so I can't see there being a problem.'

The park was busy. It was a cool but fine Sunday morning, and there were lots of people around. Ellie noted the number of children accompanied only by their fathers. She wondered how many were on access visits. Tom saw Jacob every other Sunday. It was his choice. Ellie had never raised an objection about access, realising their son needed his father, but what had started out as visits to Tom and Laura's house every weekend had dwindled to every Sunday, and had eventually dropped to every other Sunday. Tom always had a reason and Ellie couldn't exactly force him, could she? Jacob said very little on the subject, but she worried endlessly about the effect all this was having on him. He didn't deserve this. She wondered why Tom couldn't see what a wonderful son he had, and why he didn't want to spend every possible moment in his company.

'He's not here, is he, Mum? Do you think he'll come?' Jacob's face was anxious and Ellie ruffled his hair, trying to quell her anxiety. She didn't want yet another man to let Jacob down; but on the other hand, Dylan was hardly a friend, was he? She couldn't hold him to anything and she had to make sure her son realised that it had only been a casual suggestion.

'Dylan? Oh, well, he may. It doesn't really matter, does it? We're here to walk Baxter. If Dylan turns up that's very nice, but if he doesn't, we'll still have a good time, won't we?'

'But he said he'd come. He will come, won't he? He said Baxter could meet Tyson.'

Ellie closed her eyes and took a deep breath. 'Sometimes people say things, Jacob. It doesn't mean that they're deliberately lying, just that other things come up. Dylan did say that weekends are tricky for him, remember? He may have wanted to come but something cropped up that he couldn't get out of.'

'Like Dad?'

'Dad?'

'Yeah.' Jacob kicked a clump of turf and shrugged. 'Sometimes Dad says he'll pick me up but then things happen and he can't.'

Ellie swallowed. 'Yes, a bit like that. Except we hardly know Dylan, and we can't really be cross with him if he can't make it, can we?'

'I'm not cross. I'm just ...' Jacob's voice trailed off and he sighed.

Ellie — not for the first time — found herself wanting to go round to Tom's house and scream at him. He had no idea of the damage he had done.

Baxter seemed to sense her sudden anger and stood to attention, every muscle tensing. 'It's okay, Baxter,' said Jacob, patting the dog's head. Then he started to giggle.

'What is it? What are you — oh!' Ellie stared in amazement at Dylan strolling towards them. Trotting beside him was a tiny little Yorkshire terrier with a red ribbon tied on top of its head. This was Tyson?

'Morning! Sorry I'm a bit late.'

He was wearing jeans and a casual jacket over a white T-shirt. He looked much taller than he had yesterday, somehow, and leaner. The baggy jogging outfit hadn't done him justice, Ellie realised, trying not to stare at him. Baxter looked torn, his head swinging between Dylan, whom he was obviously delighted to see again, and the little dog, who was evidently crying out for further investigation.

'This is Tyson?' Ellie nodded at the little terrier and tried not to laugh, unlike Jacob who was openly finding this revelation highly amusing.

'Yeah, yeah.' Dylan ran his hand through his thick brown hair and shrugged, obviously embarrassed. 'It's a joke. An affectionate nickname because of his size. Don't be fooled, though. He's a terrier, and terriers are tough little chaps.'

'If you say so.' Ellie groaned as Baxter made up his mind what his first priority was and launched himself at Dylan, his paws landing hard on the poor man's stomach.

'Ouch! Okay, Baxter, I'm pleased to see you, too.' Dylan laughed and fussed the dog, handing Tyson's lead to Jacob with some relief as it became apparent that Baxter would settle for nothing less than two hands patting him and stroking him.

'He really likes you,' said Jacob.

'Does he? He hides it well.' Dylan managed to prise Baxter off him eventually and, almost reluctantly, the dog turned to greet Tyson. The two of them sniffed each other curiously for a few minutes, circling each other and getting their leads quite tangled in the process. Ellie noted with huge relief that they seemed quite friendly with each other, and Tyson didn't seem at all fazed by Baxter's size.

'Shall we let them have a run together?' suggested Dylan.

'You think they'll be okay?'

'Oh, yes. No problem. It'll do them good to burn off some energy. Watch Tyson try to outrun Baxter. I'll guarantee it.'

'He'll never do that,' said Jacob scornfully.

'Maybe not, but he'll try,' said Dylan with some confidence. 'He may have the body of a Yorkshire terrier, but he's got the heart of a lion. Watch him go.'

They unclipped the leads and howled with laughter as Tyson immediately streaked across the field, taking Baxter — who was too busy licking Dylan's hand to notice — totally by surprise. Once he'd realised what was happening, he looked stunned, then he turned and galloped after the little dog as if determined not to be humiliated.

'Told you,' said Dylan smugly. 'He never gives up and always takes him by surprise.'

'Him?'

'Whichever dog he's racing. They underestimate him. Kind of like the tortoise and the hare. So, young man,' Dylan said, turning to Jacob and rummaging in his jacket pocket, 'how do you fancy an ice cream? There's a van parked over by the duck pond. Always is on a Sunday. Here's some money. Get the biggest one you can afford.'

Jacob looked delighted. 'Can I, Mum?'

'Yes, of course, but you must come straight back. Where are your manners?'

'Thanks, Dylan.'

'My pleasure. Did you want an ice cream?' Dylan smiled at Ellie and she felt her tummy flutter in a very disturbing manner.

'No thanks. Shall we sit here on this bench?'

He agreed, and they sat together, watching in silence for some moments as Jacob headed off to the ice cream van and Tyson and Baxter galloped around the field.

'Quite impressive isn't he?' Ellie said at last, nodding at the dogs. 'Tyson, I mean.

Those little legs are working overtime to keep up with Baxter.'

'Baxter's playing with him. When the time's right he'll teach him a lesson and leave him way behind.'

Ellie stared at him. 'What makes you think that?'

Dylan shrugged. 'They always do. Tyson likes to challenge big dogs, but they seem to find him amusing and always end up beating him, no matter how hard he tries.'

'But he keeps trying,' murmured Ellie. 'I like that about him. No matter that the odds are stacked against him, he still believes one day he'll win the race.'

Dylan's expression softened as he studied her face. 'Sounds like you're in a race yourself, and not one that you're confident of winning.'

Ellie shook her head. 'Sorry. I don't know what made me say that. It's been a tough year.'

'I'm sorry to hear that. Still ...' He gave her a smile that melted her heart like ice cream on a hot July day. 'You have Jacob.

That's got to be worth something.'

'It's worth everything. Believe me, he's what keeps me going. Do you have children?'

'Me?' Dylan laughed. 'I'm barely fit to keep a dog.' His laughter died and he sighed suddenly. 'I'm *not* fit to keep a dog. I'm an irresponsible idiot most of the time.'

'Oh? I find that hard to believe.' Ellie realised she did. The little voice was murmuring to her that here was a decent, caring sort of person. But then, what did she know about him, really? Surely he knew his own character best? Unlike Tom, at least this man had the guts to admit he wasn't perfect. 'You seem to have quite a bond with Tyson, anyway, so you must be doing something right, and Baxter adores you. He's a very good judge of character. He hides when Angie's boyfriend comes round.'

'Why does he do that? He hasn't hurt him?' A look of anger crossed Dylan's face and Ellie shook her head reassuringly.

'Oh no, nothing like that. Just, he's not

impressed with dogs, and I think Baxter senses it. Wayne thinks Angie shouldn't have been so soft as to take him in. Or us, come to that. We're in his way, too, and he wants us gone.'

'But Angie wouldn't listen to him, surely?'

'I think Angie wants us gone, too. We've kind of outstayed our welcome. By about six months, actually.'

'How long have you been living with her?'

Ellie gave him a wry look. 'About six months.'

He raised an eyebrow then they both started to laugh.

'I don't know why I'm laughing,' said Ellie, wiping her eyes after a moment. 'Things are pretty dire and it's far from funny.'

'How come you're living with her, anyway?' asked Dylan, then held up his hands in horror. 'Sorry! Crossed a line there. You don't have to tell me anything. It's none of my business.'

Ellie turned her head and watched

Baxter and Tyson for a moment. Dylan followed her gaze and laughed again when Tyson began to yap in protest as Baxter streaked away from him, easily outrunning the little dog whose tiny legs were simply not up to the job.

'Told you. Happens every time. Poor Tyson, he never learns.'

'He will. One day.' Ellie felt over-whelmed with sadness suddenly, and was grateful when Dylan's hand rested on hers momentarily.

'Sorry,' he said, removing it almost immediately. 'Just, you looked so miserable, and I can see you've got an awful lot going on.'

He looked awkward, and Ellie tried to pull herself together and make light of the situation. 'A messy divorce, that's all. Happens to a lot of people at some point or other.'

'Tell me about it.' His voice was loaded with feeling.

'You've been through it, too?'

'Not directly. Never been married. My parents got divorced when I was very

61

young. It was horrendous. They were both still full of bitterness towards each other, even years later, and my childhood was pretty much ruined by their petty games and quarrelling. They should never have got married in the first place. Mind you, I think that's pretty much true of everyone. Marriage is a cunning plan to destroy everyone's lives, if you ask me.'

He seemed to expect her to agree, but she couldn't. 'They obviously really hurt you. You must know someone who was happily married?'

He considered for a moment. 'Yeah, a few of my mates are. But then, it's still early days. Give it a couple of years and we'll see how happy they are then.'

'What an awful way to look at the world!'

He looked surprised. 'Don't you agree?'

'Certainly not! I think marriage can be the most wonderful thing that can happen to a person. You just have to meet the right one, that's all.'

'Sure. It's a great institution, but then —'

'Who wants to live in an institution!' she finished for him, and he laughed.

'Okay, it's an oldie but goodie. Oh, hello, Baxter. You've had enough running around for now, then?'

Baxter plonked his head on Dylan's knee and gazed up at him adoringly, while Ellie tried hard not to feel offended that he was completely ignoring her. She saw Jacob walking towards them, licking his ice cream. He raised a hand and waved to her and she waved back, feeling the familiar surge of love for him.

'He really does mean the world to you, doesn't he?' Dylan's voice was quiet and Ellie turned to him in surprise.

'Of course he does. He's my son.'

'It doesn't necessarily follow.' He stroked Baxter's head for a moment in silence, then stood up. 'Come on, Tyson,' he called. 'You've let the side down enough, don't you think? Get back here now.'

Tyson took no notice, stopping to investigate a game of football that two young children were playing. Dylan called again, but Tyson may as well have been stone deaf for all the notice he took of him.

'Not very well-trained, is he?' said Jacob, sitting between Ellie and Dylan on the bench. 'Thanks for the ice cream. It's lovely.'

'Pleasure, mate. Tyson usually does as he's told. Can't understand it. Must be all the excitement.'

'Yeah, right!' Jacob's eyes twinkled with mischief.

'Are you saying you don't believe me? That's outrageous! Tyson, come here now!'

Tyson yapped excitedly and began to nudge the football away from a little boy, who promptly howled.

'Oy, mate! Is this your dog? Get it on a lead, will you? My lads are trying to play football here!' The child's father motioned to Dylan to collect Tyson, and, rather shame-faced, he went over to the little dog and clipped his lead back on.

'How embarrassing,' he confided, returning to the bench with the terrier in tow. 'Bad enough that he wouldn't behave, but now everyone knows I'm the proud owner of a Yorkshire terrier.'

'Well, you chose him, didn't you?' said Ellie in surprise.

'What? Oh, no. No. He was my mother's dog, but she passed away and ...' He swallowed. 'I guess I'm a sucker for a waif and stray, too.'

They looked at each other for a moment, then Ellie turned away. 'Have you finished that ice cream, Jacob? How about we wander over to the playground and you can go on the swings and slide for a while?'

'Are you coming, too?' Jacob asked Dylan eagerly.

Dylan hesitated for a moment, then smiled. 'Why not? I'm sure your mum can cope with two dogs for a while. I'll race you to the slide!'

5

Ice Cream

Ellie heard the car door slam and peered out of the window. It was Jacob. She watched as the little boy stood on the kerb and waved as his father's car headed down the road. She felt a lump in her throat as he hitched up his backpack and turned, resolutely, back to the house.

Switching on a bright smile, she hurried to the front door and opened it, standing aside to let the little boy into the hallway, and hastily shutting the door as Baxter, having heard Jacob's arrival, promptly bounded up to them, tail wagging furiously.

'You're back! Did you have a nice day?' She helped him as he shrugged off the backpack and eyed him anxiously. He seemed okay. His face didn't bear the usual tight, strained look that it wore most Sunday evenings as he struggled to reassure her that he was absolutely fine and he'd had a lovely day with his dad and Laura.

'It was okay. Laura made me a cake. Well, it was out of a packet, but she still had to put it in the oven. And it was nice — they let me have three slices.' He grinned at Baxter and threw his arms round the excited dog. 'Hello, boy! Did you miss me? I missed you!'

'A cake, eh? That was good of her.' Ellie hesitated, wondering if they'd broken the news to him about their forthcoming marriage. How would Jacob react when he discovered Laura was about to be his new stepmother? 'Did — did they tell you anything new?' She tried not to sound anxious, but it was difficult.

Jacob screwed up his face as he thought. 'Oh yeah! Dad's offered to do the sponsored walk with me. That's good, isn't it?'

Ellie struggled to hide her shock. The school had sent home a letter a few days ago, announcing that there was to be a sponsored walk to raise funds for educational trips, and that all children should try to take part if possible, but that they would need an adult to walk with them and as many sponsors as they could get. Ellie had suggested that Jacob take the sponsor form to Tom's and ask him and Laura if they would sponsor him, but she hadn't for a moment expected that Tom would offer to accompany his son on the five-mile walk. She felt quite hurt for a moment, but pushed the feeling aside. She was being ridiculous, and very selfish. If Tom wanted to spend additional time with Jacob, that could only be a good thing. Jacob certainly seemed to think so, anyway.

'That's very kind of him,' she said. 'Isn't he at work that day?'

'No. He said he'll take the afternoon off, just for me.'

Jacob looked quite proud of this and Ellie smiled. 'Well, I should hope so, too. We'll have to get as many sponsors as we can then, won't we?'

'I'm going to ask Dylan. He'll sponsor

68

me, won't he?'

'I'm sure he will. We'll take the form to the park next Sunday. I'll take it into work with me, too — see if I can get some of the ladies there to sponsor you. We'll soon fill that paper up with names, you'll see.'

Jacob grinned and headed into the living room, Baxter trotting beside him. 'Where's Wayne?' he whispered.

Ellie winked. 'Gone home already. They had a bit of a tiff.'

'Good,' said Jacob. 'Where's Angie, then?'

'In the kitchen,' said Ellie. 'She's making our dinner. Are you hungry?'

Considering he'd had three slices of cake, she suspected probably not, but he nodded eagerly and said, 'Yeah. Starving. I only had a banana sandwich for lunch.'

'And three slices of cake!'

'That was this morning.' Jacob rushed into the kitchen, Ellie and Baxter following. Baxter sniffed appreciatively at the smell of roast chicken and Jacob imitated him perfectly. 'Hi, Angie! That smells lovely.'

Angie, who was busy mashing potatoes in a bowl, paused in her efforts and smiled at him. 'I hope you're hungry. There are extra large portions because Wayne's had to go home. Did you have a nice time at your dad's?'

Jacob nodded. 'Yeah. He's doing the sponsored walk with me.'

'Is he?' Angie raised an eyebrow at Ellie, who shrugged. 'Well, that's good of him, isn't it?'

'Yeah. Oh, and Dad and Laura are getting married.'

Angie and Ellie exchanged glances. Ellie hadn't mentioned the fact to her cousin, having spent little time in her company recently. For the first time in ages, Angie looked like her old self, full of concern and compassion for Ellie. 'That's nice. Why don't you go upstairs and wash your hands, while I finish making dinner?'

'Okay.' Jacob turned and left the kitchen, Baxter following him like a shadow.

'Don't let that dog upstairs!' called Angie, then turned to Ellie. 'Are you okay? Did you know about this?'

'Yes. It's fine. I've come to terms with it all now. If that's what Tom wants, let him have it. What difference does it make to me now? Whether he and Laura stay together or not, there's no going back for us.'

'I'm sorry, Ellie. It must still feel like a kick in the teeth. He's a git and she's just a stupid, vain kid. She'll get sick of him soon enough, you wait and see.'

Ellie nodded. 'Probably. I was more worried about how Jacob would take it, but he doesn't seem at all bothered. I suppose that's a good thing.'

'Are you upset that Tom's doing the walk with him? That's a turn-up for the books! Never thought he'd put himself out like that.'

'Me neither. I admit, I feel a bit pushed out. But then, Jacob sees so little of him. I can't help but feel it's a good thing that Tom wants to spend more time with him. Maybe he has missed him, after all.'

'Let's just hope he doesn't let him down,' said Angie. 'Right, let's get on with this dinner. You couldn't strain the veg for me, could you? Honestly, you need to be an octopus to cook a Sunday roast. Whose bright idea was this, anyway?'

'Wayne's,' said Ellie.

They looked at each other and burst out laughing. For a short while, it was as if the arguments and tension of the last few weeks had never happened.

* * *

'I'll be glad to sponsor you, Jacob,' said Dylan, taking the pen and sponsor form from Ellie's hand. 'Cottesmore Primary, eh? I used to go there, many moons ago. It's a good school. My niece goes there, too.'

'Your niece?' Ellie was surprised. 'I didn't realise you had siblings.'

'Well, that's probably because I haven't mentioned him till now,' said Dylan with a grin.

Ellie blushed. Of course he hadn't. Why would he? Honestly, it wasn't as if they'd had any in-depth discussions, was it? 'So you have a brother?'

'Yep.' Dylan signed the form and handed it back to her.

Jacob, who was sitting on the grass playing with Baxter and Tyson, looked up. 'Can I get an ice cream, Mum?'

'Let me,' said Dylan, reaching into his jacket pocket for change.

'Oh no, honestly. You always pay. I'll get him one.'

Dylan shook his head. 'It's my treat. I make sure I have change in my pocket every Sunday, just for him. There you go, Jacob.'

Jacob looked uncertainly at his mother. She smiled. 'It's okay, Jacob. You can take it.'

'Thanks, Dylan.' Jacob took the coins and rushed off to the ice cream van. Baxter and Tyson seemed about to follow him, but Dylan was prepared and grabbed hold of their collars.

'Oh no, you don't! Come on, sit here.'

The two dogs sat patiently, allowing themselves to be stroked and fussed for a while.

'So,' said Ellie, seizing the chance to find out a little more about Dylan while she had the opportunity, 'your brother?'

'What about him?'

'Well, do you have more than one? Sisters? Older or younger?'

Dylan laughed. 'Why do I feel I'm being interviewed?'

Ellie blushed and he nudged her.

'Only joking. I just have one brother. No sisters. I'm three years older than him and he never lets me forget it.'

'So he's three years younger than you and already has a child at primary school? You have a lot of catching up to do!'

She could have clapped her hand over her mouth in horror as she realised what she'd said. He would think she was propositioning him at this rate. Was she? Of course not! She was just having a friendly chat with a nice man, that's all. *Yes, keep telling yourself that, Ellie*, she thought grimly.

'Hmm. He'll probably have a child with a child of her own before I feel able to have kids,' said Dylan.

'Really? Why are you so against having children? You're awfully good with Jacob. I think you'd make a great father.' Oh hell, she'd done it again. She ought to have a zip on that mouth of hers.

'That's what Greg says. He's my brother. He and his wife are always banging on at me to settle down and have kids.'

'But you don't want any?'

'I just think kids deserve the best, and I'm not sure I'd be up to the job.' He shrugged.

'So your brother and his wife are still together? I thought you said you didn't know any happily married couples?'

'Who said they were happy?' His eyes twinkled. 'No, to be fair, they're really good together. I don't know. I never count them, somehow. They seem like something apart. They're so happy it's sickening, but I really don't think they're typical. When I think of married couples I don't think of them, I think of — other people.'

'Like your parents?' said Ellie gently.

75

Obviously his parents' divorce had affected him very badly. Enough to put him off ever marrying or having children of his own. The thought saddened her.

'My parents didn't have a marriage. They had a war. Even after the divorce there was no surrender. Greg and I weren't children; we were grenades to be hurled between them in order to inflict as much damage on the enemy as possible. Oh well, they're both gone now. It doesn't matter anymore.'

Jacob came running back, so Ellie said nothing else on the subject, but she couldn't stop thinking about how hurt and bewildered those two little boys must have been throughout their childhood. God forbid Jacob should ever feel like that. She would do everything in her power to keep things civil with Tom, no matter how much he'd hurt her.

'Oh no you don't!' Jacob whisked his hand away quickly as Baxter made a lunge for the ice cream. Unfortunately, as he moved it to the other side of his body, Tyson took a gamble and leapt up, managing to grab a mouthful in mid-air.

'Tyson!' All three of them yelled and the little dog jumped, licking his lips guiltily. Baxter looked quite put out that he'd failed where his tiny pal had succeeded.

'Don't eat that now, Jacob,' warned Ellie, seeing her son was considering the possibility. 'You may as well let them share it and go and buy another one. Here,' she said, handing him the money. 'I don't generally think bad behaviour should be rewarded, but waste not, want not,' she said with a grin.

Jacob rushed back to the ice cream van and the two dogs fell upon the melting confection he'd left behind.

'Can't believe you did that,' said Dylan, shaking his head at Tyson as the dog sat busily licking ice cream from the fur around his mouth. 'You look so sweet and innocent, and you're nothing but a thief.'

'A cute thief, though,' said Ellie. She reached out and stroked Tyson, who immediately rolled over to have his belly tickled. She laughed and began to tickle him, then stopped, her eyes widening.

'Er, Dylan …'

He followed her gaze and was silent for a moment. 'Oh.'

'Oh, indeed. I thought you said Tyson was a boy? Quite clearly, she's a girl.'

Dylan swallowed, then put his fingers to his lips. 'Ssh, she'll hear you.'

'Who'll hear me?'

'Tyson! She doesn't know, you see. She thinks she's a boy.'

Ellie wondered if he'd gone mad. 'What the heck are you talking about?'

'She doesn't realise she's a girl. She'd be most upset to discover the truth, so we let her think she's a boy. Hence the name.'

'And how do you know all this?'

'Well, let's just say she wouldn't be interested in Baxter in any romantic fashion.'

Looking at Baxter's squashed face, which was currently spattered with ice cream, Ellie couldn't help wondering how many lady dogs would. 'You mean she's gay? You're saying you have a gay dog?'

'That's right.'

'I don't know what to say to that,'

admitted Ellie.

'I hope you're not homophobic,' said Dylan in mock indignation.

'I'm just stunned. I don't think I've ever met a gay dog before. Especially a gay dog who doesn't know it's gay but thinks it's a member of the opposite sex. Interesting.'

'I'm glad I've broadened your education,' said Dylan.

Ellie couldn't help laughing. She had no idea what he was talking about, but at least he'd relaxed and was smiling again. He'd lost all the tension that had been in his face when he'd talked about his parents. He looked a different person, and she realised that he looked extraordinarily handsome when he smiled, and that she wanted to see him smile much more. Her little voice was telling her that here, at last, was a man who might put the smile back on her own face, too.

6

A Close Encounter

Ellie had just finished hanging out the last of the washing when she heard the commotion coming from the kitchen. Wondering what on earth had happened now, she picked up the empty laundry basket and headed back indoors to find Wayne, the vein in his forehead almost popping with rage, waving a pair of jeans at Baxter, who was under the table looking, it had to be admitted, not particularly bothered. He seemed to have realised that Wayne was all hot air, and no longer concerned himself with his temper tantrums. Ellie rather admired him for it.

Angie was hanging onto Wayne's arm in a vain attempt to soothe him. She wasn't having much success by the look of it. Ellie watched in fascination as the vein throbbed and pulsed. How much longer could it continue before it burst? she wondered. She was glad Jacob was at school and didn't have to witness such a display.

'What the heck are you shouting for?' Ellie said. 'I could hear you all the way from the end of the garden.'

'That dog! Look what that dog's done now!' Wayne turned an accusing eye on her as if it were all her fault and Baxter was her responsibility. Although, come to think of it, he seemed to be more and more her responsibility these days. She was the one who fed him, cleaned his teeth and made sure he had fresh water, and she was certainly responsible for taking him for walks. Angie hadn't made the slightest attempt to for over a week at least. The novelty had well and truly worn off, and Ellie was certain it was only guilt that had prevented her from seeking a new home for poor Baxter. It was also guilt that was preventing her from coming right out and telling Ellie and Jacob to leave, too, she was sure. Well, with any luck, it wouldn't be long before they could. She had seen a flat advertised and the rent was just about affordable. What was more, the owner wasn't demanding an arm and a leg as a deposit. The only downside was, there were no pets allowed. What would happen to Baxter once they left?

As if sensing her thoughts, Baxter edged his way out from under the table and made his way slowly to her side. She put the laundry basket on the table and crouched down beside him, her arms going around him protectively. 'What's he done?'

'Are you blind? My jeans. Look at my jeans!' Wayne waved the jeans in her face and she frowned.

'Can't see anything wrong with them.'

'The pocket's torn off. Look at that!'

'Is that all? That can easily be mended.'

'And there's slobber and paw prints all over them!'

'They can be washed.' Ellie looked at him scornfully. 'Honestly, what a fuss about nothing.'

'Do you know how much these jeans

cost me? They're not your average market tat, you know. These are designer jeans. They cost me nearly two hundred quid.'

'Two hundred pounds for a pair of jeans?' Ellie bit her lip before she was tempted to tell him what an idiot he was for forking out that much for a few scraps of denim. 'How did Baxter get hold of them?'

'They were on my bedroom floor. He shouldn't have been in there. That's your fault,' said Angie accusingly. 'You've trained him to go upstairs by letting him sleep in your room. I told you not to do it.'

'And I haven't,' protested Ellie. 'Not since you mentioned it.'

'Greedy sod,' said Wayne, glaring at the dog fiercely. 'I know what you were after, mate. You knew my mints were in my pocket, didn't you? And you snaffled the lot, paper an' all. Well, you can forget about having any tea tonight.'

'Don't be ridiculous,' snapped Ellie. 'You can't not feed him just because he had a few mints. That's cruelty.'

'And eating my best jeans isn't? I

should sue you.'

'Sue me? He's not my dog!'

'May as well be,' sniffed Angie. 'He never bothers with me, does he? Only ever wants you.'

'Is it surprising? You either ignore him or yell at him. Why would he want to be around you? You should never have taken him on. You have no idea about caring for dogs and you're obviously not interested in him.'

'I was trying to do something nice!' Angie yelled. 'That's all the thanks I get. Well, I won't be so soft in the future, you can bet on that. I've learned my lesson about doing favours for people and for animals. Wish I'd never bothered with either of you. The sooner you both go, the better!'

Ellie flinched. Angie looked uncomfortable, obviously realising she'd gone a step too far. She shrugged and looked away, unable to meet Ellie's eyes.

'I'm sorry we've overstayed our welcome —' Ellie began, but Wayne butted in.

'At least you've finally realised it.

You've taken advantage for long enough. She was happy to help you out, but it's been over seven months now. You've had ages to find somewhere else. Bet you haven't even bothered looking, have you?'

'I — I may have found somewhere. I'm going to view it tomorrow before work. I'm sorry I've been such a burden on you, Angie.'

Angie murmured something but Ellie didn't catch what she said and Wayne was already pulling her back into the living room, casting a furious glare at Baxter as he went.

Ellie found she was shaking. She would never have believed that she and Angie would come to this. How on earth had things got so bad between them? She sank onto the chair and stared at Baxter as he sat, happily looking back at her, as if the whole unpleasant business hadn't touched him at all. She was glad he wasn't afraid or upset. Wayne could be a nasty piece of work, but Baxter didn't seem to let him get to him anymore. She looked at her watch. Jacob wouldn't be home from school for another couple of hours. She couldn't face sitting at home with those two until then. Besides, she thought they needed some cooling-off space.

'Come on, Baxter. Extra walk for you today.'

Baxter looked delighted by this turn of events. He'd already had a good gallop around the park that morning, tormented Tyson as usual, been treated to a biscuit by Dylan, and been made a huge fuss of by some tiny children and their mothers. The prospect of an unexpected walk was the icing on the cake, no doubt. Ellie wondered if he considered it a reward for chewing Wayne's jeans. It could be viewed as such, she supposed, and there was a wicked part of her that rather thought he'd earned it.

As they left the house, Ellie decided not to go to the park. She told herself that it had nothing to do with the little voice in her head that whispered it wouldn't be the same without Dylan. It was simply that she fancied a change of scenery. That was all.

After turning right at the top of the street instead of their usual left, she let Baxter lead the way from that point onwards, not really minding where they walked. She thought about the flat she'd seen advertised. It wasn't very big — just two bedrooms, a small kitchen, bathroom and lounge — but it looked clean. At least, it did on the photos. What it would look like in real life was another matter. The landlady had sounded quite pleasant, and she hadn't minded about Jacob. Ellie had been shocked to discover how many properties had strict "no children" rules. It was a first-floor flat, which wasn't ideal, and there was no garden, which was a shame. At least it was in a fairly pleasant area of the town, and not too far from the park. She could still take Jacob most days, either before or after school, and on weekends.

She wondered if she and Angie could repair their relationship after she left. Would Angie allow her to take Baxter for his daily walk, or would she not want Ellie anywhere near her house again? It would break Jacob's heart if he didn't see the dog after they moved. He'd grown extremely attached to him. He'd also grown attached to Dylan. As well as their regular Sunday mornings, they met up with him two or three mornings a week before school and walked the dogs together. Sometimes they'd only managed half an hour before Dylan had to rush off to work, but he always turned up when he said he would, and Jacob was really starting to believe in him. Ellie was really starting to believe in him, too. She tried not to think about what would happen if they couldn't continue their walks with Baxter. Would Dylan still be interested? What excuse would she have to carry on their meetings? She knew Jacob would miss him. She would miss him.

She was shaken from her reverie by a sudden tugging at the lead. She looked around in surprise. Where on earth were they? Baxter had taken her to an area she wasn't too familiar with. She looked at the nearest street sign. Glamis Avenue. That rang a bell. She had a vague notion of where they were, at least. It was a lovely little street, full of large detached bungalows and leafy gardens, neat hedges and wide grass verges. Very pretty.

Baxter pulled again and Ellie pulled back. 'Behave, Baxter. What on earth's got into you? Walk nicely.'

Baxter appeared oblivious to either her voice or her hand on the lead. He suddenly came to a dramatic halt, almost causing her to trip over him. 'For goodness' sake, Baxter! What are you doing?'

Baxter shot forward, pulling Ellie with him. Frantically she tightened her grip on the lead and tried to slow him down, but it was like trying to stop a runaway train. He hurtled along the pavement and she puffed along behind him, wondering what had caught his attention that was so important it made him behave this badly.

Suddenly he stopped dead, and fortunately Ellie just managed to avoid colliding with him. He was standing in front of a garden gate, looking straight ahead of him. Ellie followed his gaze and froze. Sitting on the front step of this pretty whitewashed bungalow was a beautiful cat. It had thick cream fur; a pale grey face, ears and paws; and big blue eyes. It was quite stunning, and it gave the impression that it was all too aware of that fact as it sat in the sunshine, blinking lazily now and then, and not appearing in any way concerned that a huge drooling Boxer dog was standing only yards from it, eyeballing it in a fairly alarming manner.

Nervously, Ellie wound the lead round her wrist. If Baxter somehow managed to get into this garden the cat would be history. He was panting quite frantically, every muscle straining as he pushed his nose through the wrought-iron gate and glared at the cat. Ellie grabbed hold of his collar with her other hand and tried to pull him away, but he wasn't budging. Every time she managed to move him a few inches, he summoned all his strength and moved back. The cat wasn't helping. It yawned and blinked at him quite provocatively, then stood up, arching its back as if stretching after a long sleep. Baxter growled.

The cat padded leisurely around the garden, quite obviously aware that Baxter was following its every move. It was tormenting him, no doubt about it. Ellie cursed it under her breath. It would soon get a shifty on if she lost her grip on the lead. She peered through the windows of the bungalow, hoping to catch a glimpse of someone moving around. If she could attract their attention, they might rush out and rescue the cat, and Baxter would be persuaded to leave. There was a van parked in the drive, so she knew someone was in. It was bright pink with the words "Nailed It! Manicures and Acrylics" painted on the sides.

Baxter growled again and the cat stood still and stared at him. It was too much for the dog, who hurled himself at the gate. The cat shot under the van and lay there, peering out at the trembling dog with huge blue eyes.

Ellie hauled with all her strength on the lead, and had just managed to pull Baxter's head from out of the gap in the gate when she heard a woman's voice calling from the back of the bungalow.

'Cupcake! Where are you, Cupcake? Dinner time, darling!'

The cat shot out from under the van, and before Baxter had time to react it had leapt to the top of the tall gate at the side of the bungalow and disappeared into the back garden. Ellie breathed a huge sigh of relief as Baxter visibly deflated and turned to follow her. His head hung low and he looked terribly miserable.

'Sorry, Baxter, but there's no way I could let you get hold of that cat. I know it was teasing you, but believe me, it would have been a disaster if I'd let go of your lead. And you're in enough trouble, don't you think?'

Baxter gave a big sigh and Ellie frowned. He looked suddenly awfully depressed. Did dogs get depressed? Did he know he was in the way at home and that he was skating on very thin ice? If so, he must be feeling as uncertain and unwanted as she was.

'What a pair we make, eh, boy?' She leaned forward, patting him on the back as he padded despondently towards home. Home ... Would Angie's place be his home for much longer? Would it be her and Jacob's for much longer? What on earth was going to become of them all?

7

Moving On

It was almost as if Baxter knew. Ellie managed to mop the puddle up from the kitchen floor just in time. Angie appeared, yawning, just as she put the mop and bucket back in the cupboard.

'Cup of tea, Ellie?'

Angie had been a lot more pleasant to Ellie since she had announced that she and Jacob would be moving out. The flat wasn't perfect, but over time she could decorate it the way she wanted; and with her and Jacob's things out of storage at last, it would soon feel like home.

Jacob had been upset about the move. Ellie took him to view the flat after she'd signed the tenancy agreement and handed over the deposit, and he'd looked around, obviously not impressed.

'Try to imagine it with our things in

it,' Ellie had urged him. 'Think about your bedroom decorated nicely, and all your posters on the wall, and your books and toys around you. You'll have your own bed again, Jacob! It'll be lovely when we've finished.'

He nodded, trying to be noble about the whole thing for her sake. She wanted to put her arms around him and sob. It wasn't what she'd wanted for him, but they had to make the best of things. There was no alternative.

'The park's only ten minutes away,' she told him. 'We can go there every day if you like.'

'What about Baxter?'

'What about him?'

'Can we still take him to the park? Will we still meet Dylan every day?'

Ellie swallowed. 'I — I'm not sure yet. I'll have to ask Angie. I can't see it being a problem, though. She doesn't like walking him, does she? I should think she'll be relieved if we carry on walking him for her.'

Jacob seemed to cheer up a bit after

that. Now, as Angie popped teabags in two mugs and whistled cheerfully to herself, Ellie decided it was time to make certain of the situation.

'Angie, about Baxter ...'

Angie stopped whistling. She went to the fridge and took out some milk. 'What about him?' she said eventually. 'If you're going to give me a lecture about taking him for walks and cleaning his teeth and feeding him on time, don't bother. I'm not six years old, you know. I am a responsible adult. Just because you took over everything doesn't mean I'm not capable.'

'I wasn't going to say that,' protested Ellie, although privately she had wondered. 'I was simply going to ask you if it'd be all right for me and Jacob to still take him for walks. It's not that I don't trust you to do it,' she said quickly, seeing Angie's face. 'It's just that it really cheers Jacob up. He loves Baxter so much, and he's been through such a lot already this year. I don't want to take that bit of pleasure away from him.'

Angie's face softened. 'Of course.

That's fine, Ellie. Take him for walks any time you like. Baxter's really fond of Jacob, anyone can see that. I wouldn't want to split them up.' She handed Ellie a mug of tea and took a sip of her own drink. 'So, this flat. It's okay?'

Ellie thought it was a bit late to be asking her now. They were moving in that very day and Angie hadn't so much as enquired where it was in the two weeks they'd been packing and preparing. It was as if she hadn't even known they were leaving. Baxter knew, though, Ellie was certain of it. He'd been watching them quite anxiously for days now, and stuck to their sides like glue. The puddle this morning only served to confirm Ellie's suspicions. He'd never had an accident in the house before. Thank goodness Angie hadn't seen it.

'It's not too bad.' She shrugged. 'Best of a bad bunch, really. I can make it nicer, though. A lick of paint will cheer it up, and once we get all our furniture in there I'm sure it'll be all right.'

Angie nodded. 'I'm sorry the way

things have been,' she said eventually. 'You must think I'm a total cow.'

Ellie bit her lip, wondering if she should reply honestly or not.

'Thing is,' said Angie, fortunately not waiting for a reply, 'Wayne kept going on at me. He wanted you out, and I have an awful feeling he wants to move in.'

'And you don't want him to?'

Angie hesitated. 'Wayne's all right,' she said eventually, 'but I'm not sure I could stand him actually living here. It can be a bit much sometimes.' She peered at Ellie over her mug and grinned. 'Let's just say I'm often glad when it's Sunday evening and I know he's going home.'

'Then don't let him move in with you,' advised Ellie. 'If you feel like that now, it'll only get worse. You strike me as the sort of person who needs her own space. Learn your lesson. No more waifs and strays.'

Angie's eyes filled with tears. 'I'm sorry, Ellie. I didn't mean to give you such a hard time.'

In spite of herself, Ellie put down her

mug and went over to her cousin, putting her arm around her. 'It's okay. It's hard living with other people. It was good of you to take us in. You put a roof over our heads for over eight months, and that means a lot. Thank you. I hope we can go back to being friends again now I'm out from under your feet.'

Angie sniffed and nodded. 'I hope so, too. Do you need any help today? I can put work on hold. It wouldn't be a problem.'

Ellie smiled. 'If you're sure? You could always load up the car and take Jacob's things to the flat, if you don't mind?'

'No problem. I'd like to see where you're going to be living anyway.'

⋆　⋆　⋆

Angie looked around and obviously tried to sound positive. 'Well, it's lovely and cosy,' she said, a bit too brightly.

'You'll be saying that it's compact and bijou next,' said Ellie wryly. 'I know it's small, but there's only the two of us. It'll be fine.'

Angie nodded. 'I've got some paint in the shed,' she said. 'It's a nice warm cream colour. It'd brighten up this room nicely, if you'd like it?'

'That'd be brilliant. Thanks, Angie.' Ellie had wondered how she was going to find the spare money for paint, so her cousin's offer was very welcome. At the moment the living room was painted dark red, which made it seem even smaller, and very gloomy.

'I'll drop it round for you tomorrow. What time are you at work?'

'Tomorrow? I'm on afternoons. You're sure you don't mind having Jacob if I'm asked to do evenings?'

'Told you, not a problem.'

Angie had been falling over herself all day to make amends for her behaviour. Ellie couldn't help feeling relieved. They'd been friends all their lives, and she was glad their relationship could still be saved, in spite of the tensions of the last few months. Plus, she really needed Angie's help. It was good to have someone not too far away on call in case Jacob needed picking up from school or she had to work an evening shift. Tom was worse than useless in that respect, only willing to bother with his son on alternative Sundays. Any requests for extra help with childcare were met with whining excuses.

The removal van had dropped off the bits of furniture that had been in storage ever since Ellie and Tom had given up their rented house and moved in with his mother. It felt strange seeing them again. Ellie couldn't help remembering the last time she'd seen them, and Angie seemed to sense what was on her mind.

'Still hurts?' she asked gently. 'Stupid question. This must be so tough for you.'

'Not as tough as it was,' admitted Ellie. 'Did I tell you they've set the date? Apparently they're getting married in three weeks' time.'

'No way! That was fast work! Well, it won't last five minutes,' predicted Angie confidently. 'God, he didn't waste much time, did he? When did he tell you?'

'He didn't exactly,' said Ellie. She told

Angie about the bombshell Jacob had dropped on her last Sunday, when he'd awkwardly informed her that he was going to have a new brother or sister, and his father was taking him into town the following Saturday to get him a suit as the wedding had been brought forward.

'Oh hell, and there was I giving you all that grief. I'm so sorry. You must be devastated.'

Ellie shook her head. 'Not really. Not anymore. It hurt me most that Tom wouldn't even consider having more children with me. I really didn't want Jacob to be an only child, but he was adamant one was enough. Then again, I get the distinct impression that this child wasn't exactly planned. Oh, it doesn't matter now, does it? Tom's in the past. If it wasn't for Jacob, I wouldn't have anything to do with him. He wasn't who I thought he was at all.'

'Most men aren't,' said Angie gloomily. 'Look at Wayne. All macho and tough, yet he spends more time in front of the mirror than anywhere else, wastes a fortune on hair gel and moisturiser, and has a hissy fit over a packet of mints!'

Ellie couldn't help laughing, remembering the throbbing vein in Wayne's forehead.

'I've been meaning to ask you,' said Angie suddenly. 'Who's Dylan?'

Ellie felt her face burning and knew she was blushing. Damn. 'Why do you ask?'

'I heard Jacob talking to Baxter about meeting Dylan and Tyson in the park. From what he was saying, I'm guessing — I'm hoping — that Tyson is a dog. But who on earth is Dylan?' She peered at Ellie closely. 'You're blushing! Ooh, come on! Spill the beans!'

'He's just a man we met at the park,' said Ellie. 'He walks his dog there, too, and we sort of chummed up and decided to walk them together. It's company for the dogs!' she protested as Angie gave her a quizzical look.

'Then why is your face bright red? I think someone's got a bit of a crush on this Dylan.'

'Not at all,' began Ellie. Then she grinned. 'Well, he is rather nice.'

'Really? Do tell!'

'We're supposed to be unpacking and putting all this stuff away before Jacob leaves school,' Ellie pointed out.

'Plenty of time yet, and I'll pick him up in the car. Tell you what, I'll dig out the kettle and make us a cuppa while you put the bedding on yours and Jacob's beds, then we'll sit down for ten minutes and you can tell me all about him.'

★　★　★

'He sounds really lovely,' said Angie after Ellie finally brought her up to date with the Dylan situation. 'But you left out the most important part.'

'Oh? What's that?'

'Do you fancy him?' She nudged Ellie in delight as a crimson flush spread from her chest to her forehead. 'You do! Look at you blushing again. What does he look like?'

Ellie realised she was smiling and tried, not altogether successfully, to straighten her face. 'Oh, you know. Nice.'

'Nice? What kind of a word is nice? Nice means nothing at all! Is he short or tall?'

Ellie considered, 'About the same height as Tom, I'd say. Just under six foot.'

'Fat or thin?'

'Kind of in between. Not too skinny. He runs every morning before he meets us for walks, so I suppose he's pretty fit.'

'Ooh, you want him fit,' giggled Angie. 'Fair or dark?'

'Sort of mid-brown hair, and before you ask he has grey-green eyes. And a very well-shaped mouth.'

Angie gaped at her. 'Boy, you've got it bad! So, how far have things progressed?'

'I've told you. We just walk the dogs, and we sit on the bench and talk while they play and Jacob goes on the swings. Sometimes on Sundays we feed the ducks and get an ice cream. It's no big deal.'

'But it *is* a big deal! It's quite obvious that he matters to you. Haven't you met him outside of the park?'

Ellie shook her head.

'Why ever not? Haven't you suggested

it?'

'It's not like that!' Ellie didn't know how to explain. 'He's never suggested it, either. Nothing's happened. We just chat.'

'What do you chat about?'

Ellie thought it wise not to mention all the conversations she and Dylan had had about Angie's unwelcoming attitude and how appalling Wayne was.

'About Tom and what went wrong there, about my job, about the flat. Just stuff.'

'And what about him? What does he talk about? Or is this a one-way conversation?'

'Of course not.' Ellie realised that Dylan didn't really talk about himself that much at all. He was such a sympathetic listener, she hadn't really thought about how little he'd told her of his own life. How embarrassing. He must think she was totally self-centred. She tried to remember the bits he had told her.

'He's an electrician,' she said. 'Has his own business.'

'Well, that's good news,' said Angie. 'At

least he's solvent. Where does he live?'

Ellie looked pensive. 'I don't know.' She'd asked once or twice, but he'd been surprisingly vague, now that she thought about it. Why was that? 'I should think he doesn't live far from here. After all, he goes to the park pretty frequently.'

'Married? Any kids?'

At least Ellie could answer that with confidence. 'No. Definitely not.'

'Brilliant! So no baggage.'

'He doesn't believe in marriage,' said Ellie, suddenly deflated. 'And he says he's not responsible enough to have kids.'

Angie looked disappointed. 'Oh. Not so good.' Then she brightened. 'Still, at least he's honest, and that counts for a lot. He's probably just not met the right woman before now. I reckon things will change once you two get together.'

'But we're not getting together,' sighed Ellie. 'We just walk our dogs together. There's been no suggestion of anything else.'

'What, none at all? No lingering looks, no touchy-feely?'

'Not really.' Although there had been moments … times when Ellie had thought something could have happened, was about to happen, but they always came to nothing. Surely, if Dylan were interested in her he would have done something about it by now?

'Maybe he's thinking the same about you,' said Angie when she voiced her opinion. 'One of you has got to stop being so polite and make a move, and it may just as well be you. Go for it! These are exciting times! A new home and maybe a new man. Time to put the past behind you, Ellie. Leave Tom behind and move on.'

Ellie looked around the living room and tried to visualise it painted cream and adorned with the photographs and pictures and ornaments that had been packed away for so long. She could make it a home, she knew she could. It would take a bit of money and a bit of effort, but eventually she and Jacob would settle and life would take on a new normality.

A new home had been her main concern for so many months, but now she had it, and making it comfortable didn't seem like such a challenge after all. But a new man? That would take a bit more courage, and Ellie wasn't sure she had enough for the task.

8

True to Form

'So you're settling in all right?' Dylan handed Jacob his ice cream money, ruffled his hair and warned him to come straight back, then he turned back to Ellie. 'The flat's okay? No horrific discoveries?'

Ellie laughed. 'Like what?'

'You know. Mice, mould in the bathroom, a creepy neighbour?'

Ellie scooped Tyson onto her knee, retying the ribbon, which was coming loose, on the top of the little dog's head. 'Thankfully, no. Haven't even seen the neighbours, the flat is totally mould-free, and, please God, we don't have mice. I don't think I'd still be living there if we did.'

'That's a relief. I was worried,' he said, patting a panting Baxter.

'Were you?' Ellie's stomach fluttered. It was the perfect moment to say something, put the question to him at last. Were they moving towards something? Was this relationship going anywhere? Or were they just friends who walked their dogs together in the park most days?

'Of course. Jacob wasn't happy about leaving Angie's, was he, and he's already been through so much. I'd hate to think he'd be unhappy, living in some dingy flat somewhere. I'm glad it's decent.'

'Oh. Oh yes, no need to worry.' Ellie tried hard to sound positive, though the disappointment was seeping its way through her bones. She should ask, but she couldn't make herself do it. He'd never given her any real indication that he was interested in her romantically, and if she said something she may just embarrass him, scare him off. She may never see him again, and she didn't think she could bear that. But, just sometimes, he would look at her with an expression in those beautiful grey-green eyes that quite took her breath away. At moments like that, she could almost imagine that he had feelings for her. But it wasn't worth the risk. It could all be wishful thinking. He'd said nothing, and until he did … 'I've just painted the living room. Angie gave me some cream paint and it looks much brighter now.'

'Angie gave you the paint? Wow! That was good of her.' He pushed Baxter's paws off his knee and scolded him gently as he tried to jump up again.

Ellie smiled at his sarcastic tone. 'Actually, she's been lovely since we moved out. Quite her old self. She even came round and helped me paint. Things are practically the same between us as they used to be.'

'That's good. You've forgiven her, then?'

'Forgiven her? For what?'

'For making you feel so unwelcome.'

Ellie shrugged. 'She was struggling. Wayne was making demands on her and putting pressure on her to evict us. And besides, she's used to living alone. It was tough having me and Jacob there, invading her space. I can't forget that she put a roof over our heads when we needed it most. I'll always be grateful for that. I don't know what we'd have done without her. There's nothing to forgive.'

'You're a very special person, Ellie,' he said softly.

'Me? Nothing special about me.' She retied Tyson's ribbon for the second time, though it didn't need it.

'But there is. You're so forgiving. Not just of Angie, but of Tom. After everything he put you through, you still encourage him to see his son, and I've never once heard you bad-mouth him to Jacob.'

Ellie was shocked. 'Of course not! Tom's his father! Jacob doesn't need to hear any negative stuff about his dad. He's been through enough. I'm trying to keep everything as painless and smooth as I can for him. Any mother would do the same.'

He shook his head. 'No they wouldn't, Ellie. Believe me.'

'I'm sorry. I forgot.' He looked so sad for a moment that she longed to reach out and touch his face and had to force herself not to. 'So, the sponsored walk is tomorrow. Is your niece taking part?'

'What?' He looked baffled at her sudden change of subject for a moment, then smiled. 'Oh, yes. I think she's doing a shorter route than Jacob, though. She's in pre-school. She's only four and they're only going halfway and then turning back. Can't expect those tiny tots to do the full five miles.'

'Oh bless her. Is your brother walking with her?'

Dylan shook his head. 'My sister-in-law's going with her. Greg's got to work and he's not sure he'll be back in time. Are you going along?'

'I'll be popping along later to be there at the finishing line, of course. I'm really hoping Laura isn't there.'

'Is it likely?'

Ellie frowned. 'Not really. I don't think sponsored walks are Laura's thing. Although she's going to have to get used to doing stuff like that.'

'Oh?'

Ellie hesitated, but there seemed no reason not to confide in him. 'She's pregnant. They're bringing the wedding forward for obvious reasons.'

'Oh, Ellie. I'm sorry.'

'Don't be. Honestly, I'm fine. As long as Tom doesn't push Jacob further out of his life to make room for the new baby, it really doesn't matter.'

'I'm sure that won't happen. He's doing this sponsored walk, isn't he? That must mean he really wants to spend time with Jacob. He didn't have to do it, after all. Good sign, huh?'

'Yes, absolutely.' She put Tyson back on the ground as Jacob came back. 'Shall we let these two go for a run now? I could do with stretching my legs, actually.'

'Sure,' Dylan agreed. 'I know Jacob may be exhausted after his exertions tomorrow afternoon, but do you still want to meet up here on Sunday morning before he goes to his dad's, and we could all feed the ducks? I've not done that in a while.'

She smiled. 'I'd love to,' she said. It felt

115

like he'd offered her the world. She stood up, then pulled a face as her mobile rang. 'Just a moment.' She noted the name on the screen and frowned. What did Tom want? She wandered a little away from Dylan and Jacob and answered the call. 'Tom? What can I do for you?'

'Ellie, I'm really sorry but I won't be able to do the walk with Jacob tomorrow.'

'You've got to be kidding me! Why not?'

'It really can't be helped. Laura's not well. She's got really bad morning sickness and I can't leave her like this, not in her condition. I mean, I feel awful about it, but what can I do? You'll be okay to take him, won't you?'

'Luckily for you, I don't have a shift tomorrow,' she snapped. 'What would have happened if I was working? Honestly, Tom, you should have given us more warning. Anyway, Laura might be feeling better tomorrow.'

'I doubt it. I can't make a promise I can't keep, and I really don't think I'll be there, so it's best I tell you now, isn't it? Be reasonable. Anyway, I have to go.

Tell Jacob I really am sorry, and I hope he does the walk in record time.'

'What about the day after? If Laura's so unwell, should I tell him he's not going to yours this weekend? I don't want him all packed and ready to go and then you cancel on him at the last minute.'

'Oh no, I should think she'll be okay by then. I'll let you know if not. Bye, Ellie.'

She ended the call and shoved the phone back in her jacket pocket. Now she'd have to break the news to Jacob that his father wouldn't be accompanying him on the sponsored walk after all. So much for Tom spending extra time with Jacob. She should have known it was too good to be true.

'Problem?' Dylan looked at her curiously, but she shook her head. No reason to spoil Jacob's morning. He loved their trips to the park with Baxter, Dylan and Tyson. She would break it to him gently when they got home.

9

The Walk

The school playground was packed. Crowds of children, clearly overexcited and eager to get moving, milled around, while parents tried to calm them down and muttered about needing a cigarette. Members of staff strutted round, issuing instructions and waving bits of paper, while their pupils giggled at the novelty of seeing their teachers in jeans and trainers, rather than their usual smart school clothes.

'The route is clearly signposted,' called the headmaster after his staff had managed to marshal everyone into some sort of order and had called for silence. 'There will be a refreshment table at Belvedere Close, where you'll all be able to get drinks and pause for breath. The pre-school children will turn back to the school just after that point, at Winthorpe Crescent. We feel that's quite far enough for little legs. The rest of you will continue to follow the signs, heading up Sunningdale Street and then along Northolme Drive, Penshurst Road, Seaton Avenue, Richmond Lane and back down Swanland Street to the school. There will be teachers dotted along the route if you need any help. May I suggest that the little ones use the toilet before we start? Also, if any of you grown-ups feel the need to avail yourself of the facilities, please do so now.'

'Do you need the loo, Jacob?' whispered Ellie. He nodded and headed into the school building towards the toilets. Ellie sat on the step waiting for him to return.

'Ellie?'

She looked up, squinting against the sunshine, and shielded her eyes with her hand. She blushed as she saw Dylan standing there, looking down at her. He was looking quite gorgeous in faded jeans, a grey T-shirt and a leather jacket, and he was hand-in-hand with a cute little blonde girl who was eyeing her curiously.

'Oh, hello. What are you doing here?'

'I might ask you the same question. Are you with Jacob? I thought you were coming a bit later on for the finish?'

Ellie sighed and stood up, brushing the rear of her jeans. 'Tom couldn't make it after all, so here I am!'

'Ah.' He gave her a sympathetic look. 'Sorry to hear that.'

'Yeah, well, there you go. Seems Laura's not feeling too well, so he didn't feel able to leave her. Who's this little poppet?'

'My niece, Lucy.' Dylan smiled down at the little girl, who beamed back at him. 'Her mum had a bit of an accident yesterday, so guess who got roped in to do the walk with her?'

'Oh no, I'm sorry to hear that. Is your mummy okay?' Ellie asked.

'Mummy hurt her foot,' said Lucy solemnly. 'It's gone all blue and fat. She can't get her shoe on anymore.'

'Oh dear.'

'Daddy says it's her own fault,' the

child informed her.

Ellie bit her lip, trying not to smile. 'Well, I hope she gets better soon.'

'She can't walk properly and she keeps pulling faces and saying "ow" and swearing a lot.'

'All right, Lucy. We don't need the details.' Dylan sighed.

'She's a real cutie,' whispered Ellie. 'What happened to her mum?'

'Kate wanted to get up into the loft,' he murmured. 'Greg told her to wait till he got home that evening and he'd do it and she could hold the ladder, but she decided to go ahead anyway. To make matters worse, she didn't even get the step ladder, but just balanced on a chair. Stupid. I mean, I love Kate, but honestly, it could have been really serious. Still, on a positive note, I don't think she'll try that again.' He smiled and waved as Jacob came running out of the school building. 'Okay, mate? Are we doing this thing, then?'

'You're doing the walk?' Jacob's face lit up. 'Brilliant. Who's this?' He looked suspiciously at the little girl who was now clinging possessively to her uncle.

'This is my niece, Lucy. She's in Miss Rawson's class.'

'Oh, she's one of the babies,' said Jacob dismissively. 'She'll only be going halfway. We're doing the full five miles, aren't we, Mum?'

'We certainly are,' said Ellie, rolling her eyes at Dylan. 'Can't wait.'

Dylan winked at her and she felt her tummy flutter in a very teenage-crush fashion. She hadn't felt like that for such a long time — not since she'd first met Tom, in fact. Maybe not even then.

They all set off finally, and it seemed only natural that she and Dylan would walk together. Jacob and Lucy walked in silence, seemingly reluctant to make friends. Jacob looked a bit embarrassed to be seen with a baby, and Lucy was viewing Jacob with some suspicion, much to Ellie's and Dylan's amusement.

'Good job you weren't at work,' Dylan said. 'Which supermarket do you work in, by the way?'

'Maister's. Do you ever shop there?'

'Sometimes. It's quite upmarket, isn't it?' He grinned at her. 'Bit too posh for the likes of me.'

'It's not the cheapest supermarket there is,' she admitted. 'I wouldn't shop there if I didn't work there, but I do get a discount, so it's worth it for some stuff.'

'Are you working tomorrow?'

'No. They're pretty good there and try to work around Jacob. I rarely work weekends — sometimes I work on the Sundays he visits Tom, but they mostly fit my shifts in with school hours. Kylie, who does the rota, has kids herself and is really understanding. I can't complain. What about you?'

'What about me?'

'You said you were an electrician. Do you work for a company or for yourself?'

'Myself. I used to work for Claxton's but then I thought, why am I working to make them richer? It seemed a better idea to work for myself. Not as simple as that, as it turned out, and it took me a few years to build up the business, but

123

it's doing okay now. I manage to pay the mortgage and the bills, and I have a bit left over at the end of the month, so I guess I can't complain either.'

'We're very easily pleased,' she said, her eyes twinkling.

'It seems so. Although I think I'm getting rather more choosy as I get older.'

'Oh?'

He wasn't smiling. In fact, he looked quite pensive. Ellie wondered what he was thinking.

'Are we there yet?' Lucy demanded.

'Of course not,' said Jacob. 'Honestly, we've hardly started.'

'All right, Jacob. Just remember, her legs are a lot smaller than yours,' Ellie rebuked him gently.

'Can't you remember what it was like when you were five?' said Dylan.

'Dad lived with us then,' said Jacob. 'We had a house of our own, but then we had to go and live with Grandma. I don't know why. But Grandma didn't really want us there, and I didn't like it anyway.'

'I'm sure your grandmother was

pleased to have you,' said Dylan.

'She wasn't, was she, Mum?' said Jacob. 'I don't care anyway. She smelt funny and she made me eat broccoli. I don't like broccoli.'

'I don't like broccoli either,' said Lucy with some feeling. 'It's yuck.'

'Yeah, it is,' said Jacob. 'Who wants little trees on their plate?'

Lucy giggled. 'They *are* little trees! I said they were, but Mummy said they weren't.'

'Well they are. You were right,' said Jacob. He moved in front of Dylan and fell into step beside Lucy. 'Where do you live? Does your dad live with you?'

'Of course he does,' said Lucy, sounding surprised. 'I live in a nice house, and Daddy says we've got the smartest garden in the street — doesn't he, Uncle Dylan?'

'Yes, he does. Frequently,' said Dylan. He grinned at Ellie. 'Seems like they've decided they quite like each other after all,' he murmured.

They walked together, talking about

the school, about their jobs, admiring houses that they passed, and discussing Ellie's plans for the flat, while Jacob and Lucy chattered together. Before they knew it they were at Belvedere Close, and saw the tables ahead of them along the grass verges.

'Orange juice!' squealed Lucy. 'Can I have one, Uncle Dylan?'

'Of course. Jacob, do you want one, too?'

'Yes please, Dylan,' said Jacob.

'Ellie? Orange juice, lemon barley water, or blackcurrant squash?'

'Barley water, please.' Ellie took the plastic cup gratefully and gulped the cold liquid down. It was soothing on her throat, and she realised she hadn't noticed how hot she'd been feeling. The sun was beating down quite fiercely now. Funny how she'd been so absorbed in their conversation that the heat hadn't bothered her.

Lucy and Jacob sat on the grass verges and began to pick daisies along with several other children. Parents milled around, drinking juice and agreeing that a good breeze would be very welcome.

Dylan finished his drink and took their empty plastic cups back to the table. Ellie sank onto the grass verge, a little apart from the children, and watched him as he made easy conversation with the teachers who were pouring the drinks. He drew a few admiring glances from some of the women who were standing nearby, and Ellie fought down a pang of jealousy. Honestly, what was wrong with her! He didn't belong to her, and she had no right to feel jealous. He turned his head and gave her a beautiful smile. She felt her stomach flip over and realised she was smiling back. For a moment they gazed at each other, and the crowds around them faded into the background. There was just the two of them, and Ellie knew in that moment that she was lost.

He came and sat beside her, saying nothing. Nervously she plucked at the grass, and then felt his hand upon hers. She froze, her heart pounding with excitement and nerves. Slowly she lifted her gaze to meet his and saw the same emotions reflected in those grey-green eyes. His fingers softly stroked hers, and then his hand cupped her hand and he squeezed it gently. She squeezed back, and had to suppress the desire to leap upon him. His eyes were burning into hers, then his gaze dropped to her mouth. He moved very slightly nearer to her, and she felt his breath hot on her cheek. Her eyes closed. He was going to kiss her. She could almost feel the brush of his lips on her skin. She waited in an agony of impatience.

'Right, I think it's time we were on our way!' Mr Colbeck clapped his hands and there was a general grumbling and muttering. Ellie's eyes flew open in shock and Dylan leapt back as if he'd been burnt.

'Lucy! Jacob! Time to get walking again.' He stood up, reaching for his niece's hand. She clambered to her feet, pulling a face at the effort.

'Are we going home soon? I'm hot,' she wailed.

'We'll be heading back in a minute,' he promised her. He didn't look at Ellie and she wondered if he was regretting his actions. The thought scared her. Had it all been a horrible mistake on his part?

'I'm not tired at all,' Jacob announced, taking Ellie's hand. 'But I'm a lot bigger than Lucy. You'll be going back to the school soon,' he told her. 'Don't worry.'

She nodded, and they began to walk again. Ellie had no idea what to say. What had just happened? Was she imagining things? Had Dylan really been about to kiss her, or was it all in her head? He still hadn't said anything, and she was feeling totally confused. The relentless sun beating down on her head wasn't helping. She should have brought a sun hat.

'Daddy's here! Look, Uncle Dylan! Daddy's here.'

Ellie and Dylan looked up and Ellie saw a man of similar build and colouring to Dylan standing at the bottom of the road. He raised a hand and waved, but his other hand was clutching a lead.

'He must have finished work on time,' muttered Dylan.

Ellie looked at him in surprise. He

didn't seem particularly pleased about it.

'He's brought Tyson,' observed Jacob. 'Look, Lucy, Tyson's come to see you.'

'Who's Tyson?' said Lucy, sounding puzzled.

Jacob laughed. 'That dog there,' he said, pointing to her father. 'Look, your dad's got him.'

Lucy pulled a face. 'That's not Tyson,' she said scornfully. 'That's Mitzi, Mummy's dog.'

'Mitzi?' Ellie stared at Dylan, who was looking extremely uncomfortable. 'Who's Mitzi? What's she talking about? I thought that was Tyson and I thought she was your dog?'

'Yes, well, I can explain ...'

'Can you? Go on then.'

'Daddy!' Lucy let go of Dylan's hand and ran into her father's arms.

He scooped her up, laughing. 'Hello, angel. You made it then. Aren't you a clever girl? We can head back to the school now. I'll walk with you. Mitzi and I will keep you both company.' He nodded at Dylan. 'Thanks for stepping in, bro.

You're a star.' He smiled at Ellie, his eyes full of curiosity. She tried to smile back but couldn't. Her stomach was churning. What the hell was going on? Why had Dylan lied about Tyson?

Greg looked uncertainly between Ellie and Dylan, obviously sensing a problem. 'Er, I'll start walking Lucy back, Dylan. Catch up when you can,' he said, taking his daughter's hand and following the crowd of pre-school children and their parents down Winthorpe Crescent. The older children were making their way towards Sunningdale Street.

Jacob tugged at Ellie's hand. 'Come on, Mum, or we'll be last.'

'Jacob, you go on. I'll catch you up in a moment,' she promised him.

He frowned, looking from her to Dylan and back again. 'Are you all right, Mum?'

'I'm fine. I just want to talk to Dylan about something. I won't be long. Stick with the crowd, okay? See, little David Eastwood's there with his mum. Walk with them till I get to you. I'll only be a minute.'

Jacob hesitated, then ran after David. Ellie watched, making sure that David's mum was keeping an eye on them both, then turned back to Dylan. 'So what's going on?'

He ran his hand through his hair, as she'd noticed him do before when he was stressed. 'I know it looks bad, but it really isn't. I just got caught up in something I couldn't get out of. That morning when we first met — remember?'

'Of course I remember.' She would never forget it.

'You sort of assumed that I had a dog, and I — I went along with it. I'd been sounding like such a know-it-all and I thought you'd think I was an arrogant git, giving you all this advice and not actually owning a dog myself. I told you about Tyson because he's one of my mate's dogs. He's a bull terrier and as macho as they come. Lee only got him a couple of weeks ago from a rescue centre and I guess he'd stuck in my mind. Then, when you suggested I bring him for a walk with you all, I was kind of stuck. I should have admitted everything then, but I was so embarrassed — and besides, I really wanted to meet up with you all. So I agreed, thinking I could borrow Tyson and bring him with me. Trouble was, when I asked my mate, he told me it would never work, because although Tyson is brilliant with people, he's a nightmare around other dogs. I didn't want him attacking Baxter and causing mayhem in the park, so I had to think of something else. Unfortunately, the only other dog I could think of was Mitzi. I had to throw myself on Kate's mercy and tell her everything. She told me I was an idiot but she let me borrow the dog, and that's why I was a bit late that first morning, and why I had to make up all that rubbish about Mitzi being gay.'

'Wouldn't it have been easier to just admit the truth?'

'Absolutely one hundred per cent, yes.' He shook his head. 'I'm a prize idiot and a terrible liar. I really am sorry, Ellie. I found myself panicking when you realised she was a girl, and I just couldn't believe the stuff I was saying.' He took her hand and squeezed it. 'Forgive me?'

She wanted to. Really badly. But the memory of Tom and his endless lies made her reluctant to do so. 'It's just that ...' Her voice trailed off. How could she explain it? He would never understand.

'It's just that Tom lied to you all the time, and now you're worried that I'm the same.' So he did understand, after all. The thought was comforting, but even so ...

'Are you?' Her voice was little more than a whisper. 'I don't know what's going on between us. Where is this heading?' Well, at least she'd finally had the guts to ask. She realised she was trembling, and that he was still holding her hand.

He stared at her for a long moment, then let it go. 'I'm not Tom, Ellie. Really I'm not.'

'That doesn't answer my question. In fact, it doesn't answer either of them.'

He stuck his hands in his jacket pockets and looked around helplessly. 'I have to get back to Lucy and Greg. I have to finish the walk or it doesn't count. Will you still meet me tomorrow morning? We can feed the ducks and we'll talk.'

'I — I suppose so.'

'Thank you, Ellie.' He looked anxious and rather sad as he turned and headed after Lucy and his brother. Ellie wondered what the hell was going on in his mind and why he couldn't give her a straight answer. She supposed he might be able to do so tomorrow at the park. She pushed away the thought that it would give him a whole night to come up with some plausible story. He'd said he wasn't like Tom, and the little voice in her head was urging her to believe him. She wanted so badly to listen to it. She was in too deep, and she couldn't bear to go through all that again.

10

A Question of Trust

Ellie barely slept that night, unlike Jacob, who slept solidly from around eight o'clock in the evening till almost eight o'clock the following morning. He was obviously exhausted. Maybe she should take him on a five-mile walk every day, she thought, sipping her tea and wondering if she should wake him up or leave him for another half hour. Tom hadn't been in touch, so obviously Laura was well enough for Jacob to visit. He was usually collected at around ten thirty, so if they wanted to meet Dylan in the park they would have to hurry.

She took another gulp of her tea and considered what had happened between her and Dylan. There was no denying the chemistry between the two of them. It wasn't just the sunshine that had made her so hot and bothered yesterday, and she knew that he'd felt the same. If only he hadn't told those stupid lies about Tyson.

Yet, did it really matter? When she'd first met Tom, she'd had an uncomfortable feeling about him immediately, and the little voice had been nagging away at her right from the start. She hadn't had that feeling with Dylan. On the contrary, she'd felt safe with him from their first meeting. The little voice told her that here was someone she could trust. Had she been so wrong about him?

She didn't want to be betrayed again, but was telling a few white lies about a dog really the same as the stuff Tom had lied about? Or should she draw a line in the sand right now and say even one lie was one too many, and it was over before it had begun? But then again, Dylan had said he'd wanted to meet up with them, and that was why he'd pretended to have a dog. Didn't that say something? Didn't that tell her that he'd been attracted to her right from the beginning, just as she'd

137

been attracted to him? Didn't that count for anything?

She wished she wasn't at work that afternoon. She thought she had a head-ache coming on, and wasn't in the mood for grouchy customers and miserable colleagues who'd be moaning that they hated working Sundays, especially summer Sundays, when the sun was shining and everyone else would be having barbecues or heading to the coast to sunbathe and swim. Kylie had been deeply apologetic when she'd called earlier that morning.

'I wouldn't ask, Ellie, you know that, but Suzie's rung in sick with sunburn, and Daisy and Jen aren't answering their phones. Bet they're clearing off to the coast for the day. Mind you, I can't blame them. I know it's Tom's weekend with Jacob, so I was wondering if you could do a few hours this afternoon? I'd really appreciate it.'

She'd hardly been able to say no when Kylie had done her so many favours, but it had just about put the tin hat on a pretty rubbish weekend. She heard Jacob moving about upstairs and stood up to make his breakfast. Luckily, his bag was already packed. They'd have to be quick if they wanted to go to the park and then get back in time for Tom's arrival.

She froze as the phone beeped, just as she'd opened the cereal packet. No doubt this was Tom, cancelling Jacob's visit. She banged the box of Cheerios on the worktop and snatched up her phone, glaring at the screen and practically daring Tom to have the nerve to disappoint his son yet again.

But the message wasn't from Tom. Ellie caught her breath as she realised that she'd received her very first message from Dylan. They'd exchanged numbers in case either of them ever needed to cancel or let the other know they were going to be late to the park, but they'd never actually made use of them before. She trembled, wondering what he was going to say to her. A part of her was bursting with excitement, and she tried to push those feelings down. She was acting like a teenager with a first crush. It was embarrassing. Still, she shook as she tapped the screen, hoping against hope that it was some sort of loving message — some declaration of his feelings for her. Her heart sank as she read the text.

"Really sorry, Ellie. I can't make it today. Something's come up. I promise we'll talk soon. Dylan xx"

What had come up? What was so important that he'd cancel the meeting that he seemed so desperate to have with her yesterday? And, more importantly, what did those two kisses mean? She tried to think. If you put one kiss, it was just ordinary, wasn't it? The sort of thing you'd put on anyone's text. But two meant something quite different. Or did it? She really couldn't remember now, and knew she would drive herself insane thinking about it if she carried on like that, so she pushed all thoughts of Dylan away. For all of five seconds.

'Morning, darling. How are you feeling this morning? Are your legs aching?'

Jacob looked puzzled. 'No. Why?'

Ellie smiled. 'Just me, then. My bones

are a lot older than yours, I guess. Here's your cereal. You've had a nice long sleep. You don't have to hurry, by the way, because we're not going to the park this morning.'

Jacob looked bitterly disappointed. 'Why not? What about Baxter?'

'I'll ask Angie to take him today. Dylan can't make it so I think I'll have a nice easy morning for a change and chill out before work.'

'Why can't he make it?' demanded Jacob, spooning cereal into his mouth.

Ellie pulled a face. 'Don't speak with your mouth full, Jacob. And I have no idea. I didn't ask. It's really none of our business, is it?'

'Are you and Dylan arguing?'

She looked at him in surprise. 'Of course not. What made you say that?'

'You looked very cross yesterday, and you made me go on without you, which usually means you want to talk to somebody without me hearing, and that usually means a row. Well, it does with Dad, anyway, so it probably does with

141

Dylan, too.'

'No, no, Jacob,' she protested. 'We didn't row, I promise you. We just have some stuff to sort out and that has nothing to do with not going to the park this morning.'

'Really?'

'Really. Now how about we take half an hour and watch some television before we get ready?'

★ ★ ★

'It's only a little white lie, Ellie.' Angie's eyes were warm with understanding as she put down her coffee and squeezed her cousin's hand. 'I know what you're thinking, but you can't judge all men by Tom.'

They were in the Beehive Café on the High Street. It was Wednesday afternoon, and Ellie had heard nothing from Dylan all week. She had tried to be philosophical about it, telling herself that he was a busy man and something must have come up, but she wasn't convinced. He'd behaved very oddly at the sponsored walk, and then she'd seen nothing of him since. She couldn't help feeling hurt.

Angie had popped into Maister's for a few things, just as Ellie was finishing her shift. It had apparently taken only seconds for her to ascertain that her cousin was feeling pretty low, and she'd suggested they go for a coffee in town. Ellie was too fed up to argue, although she'd promised herself that she'd go straight home and get on with stripping the kitchen wallpaper, which she frankly couldn't stand a moment longer, it was so drab. The whole flat felt drab. She knew in her heart of hearts that no amount of paint or pretty cushions was going to make it the kind of home she'd wanted for herself and Jacob. She missed having a garden and she knew Jacob did, too. She hated the small windows, the cheap carpet, the old-fashioned bathroom suite and the ancient kitchen units. She hated the gas fire on the wall and the electric cooker that had seen better days. The thought of spending years living there pulled her down. She couldn't look on the bright side anymore. Nothing was right.

In spite of herself, she agreed to go to the café with Angie. Better to spend an hour or so there in bright, cheerful surroundings than be at home. Left to her own devices, she knew she would only brood, and that was the worst thing she could do.

'I reckon it's a good sign, anyway.'

Ellie's eyes widened. 'How can the fact that he lied to me be a good sign?'

'Well, think about it. He obviously fancied you like mad from the moment he saw you, or why would he make up a dog as an excuse to walk with you every day? He's gone to a whole lot of trouble to spend time with you. I'd be flattered.'

'Would you? I suppose ... But then, why did he cancel our meeting the next day? Why haven't I heard a word from him since?'

Angie considered. 'Maybe he's just embarrassed. He must have felt so cornered when his brother turned up with the dog in front of you all, and imagine how stupid he felt having to confess the truth. Bet he's worrying himself sick, especially since he knows how you feel about being lied to. Give him the benefit of the doubt.'

Ellie sighed. Was Angie right? Was she making something out of nothing? Maybe there was a reason for Dylan's odd behaviour after all. Maybe he did have a lot of work on, or maybe he really was too embarrassed to meet her. Maybe she should call him; smooth things over?

She tried to think about something else. 'How are things with you and Wayne? Any progress on the moving in situation?'

Angie pulled a face. 'He's practically moved all his stuff in without even asking me. I can't move in that bathroom. My God, he's vain! You should see the bottles and cans and jars on the shelves. No room for my products. And it gets worse.'

'Really?' Ellie wasn't sure she wanted to know. How much worse could it be?

Angie took a mouthful of coffee and seemed to consider where her loyalties lay. She apparently decided they didn't lie with Wayne, which Ellie thought didn't bode well for their future.

'You know he used to play football for Harpington United?'

'Did he? No, I didn't know.' Ellie was quite surprised. Harpington United were the town's football team, and although they weren't exactly premier league, they were doing quite well, having recently been promoted to the champions league.

'Not the main team, of course. The under twenty-one squad. I'm going back a few years.'

'Aren't you just,' murmured Ellie.

'He could have been as good as Beckham, he says, until a knee injury put paid to his career. Anyway, it turns out that he's got a whole stack of memorabilia from those days. I mean badges, kit, medals, newspaper cuttings, a signed photo of him getting a hug from the club mascot. Honestly, a great big whacking picture of him and a six-foot badger. Why would anyone want to keep that?'

'A six-foot badger?'

'The club was sponsored by Badger's Jam.'

'Oh, of course.' Now it all made sense, thought Ellie, taking another sip of her coffee.

'His prize possession is his scrapbook. He's got everything that was ever printed about his football career in there. Photos, press reports, programmes. It's sickening. The worst of it is, he expects me to put it all on display. He wants to buy a big glass cabinet and stick the whole lot in the living room so that everyone gets to see how wonderful he was.'

'And you're not keen?'

Angie looked aghast. 'Of course I'm not keen! Would you be? Mind you, there is one benefit to his fanaticism. He's going to have to behave himself for the rest of his life, or else. Any sign of a wandering eye and I'll be making a bonfire of the lot, quicker than you can say matches. And I don't mean football matches.'

'You're evil!' said Ellie, trying not to laugh.

'Yeah, it has been said.' Angie looked around. 'Do you fancy another latte?'

Ellie checked her watch. 'No, I'd better

get off. I have to collect Jacob from school.'

'Do you want a lift?'

'No, it's fine. I can walk there in time. Might do me good to stretch my legs, get some fresh air. I need to clear my head.'

Angie winked at her. 'Cheer up, eh? Bet this time next week you'll be laughing at all these doubts and worries you're having.'

'Maybe.' Ellie smiled. 'Thanks for the coffee, Angie. I really appreciate it.'

'No problem. I'm glad to get out of the house for a bit, truth to tell. Working from home has its good points, obviously, but sometimes I feel I can go a bit stir crazy.'

'I'll pop round in the morning and take Baxter for a walk. How's he doing?'

'Missing you and Jacob. He's pining, and nothing I do or say is cheering him up,' Angie confessed. 'It's a shame you couldn't have him in that flat. He much prefers your company to mine.'

'Wayne's okay with him?'

'I think they've come to a mutual agreement. They basically ignore each other entirely. It's like they refuse to acknowledge the other's existence. It's almost funny.'

Ellie laughed. 'Sounds like you've got quite a lot to deal with yourself. I'll be round about nine, after I drop Jacob off at school. I'll take him out on Saturday, too. I promised Jacob that we could go back to the park, though I can't say I'm looking forward to that.'

'It'll all come right in the end, Ellie. Promise.' Angie scooped up her handbag and hugged her cousin. 'See you tomorrow morning. Give my love to Jacob.'

They parted outside the café and Ellie turned and headed in the direction of Jacob's school. She wondered if he would mind helping her strip the kitchen walls when they got home. It would give them both something to do, at any rate, and was better than staring at the television all evening. What could they have for dinner? She thought she had some pork chops in the fridge. Maybe he'd like those? Or she could call at the butcher's and get some sausages and do some mashed potatoes with them. He loved sausages and mash. It was probably his favourite meal. He deserved cheering up. Ellie knew he was missing their walks in the park with Dylan and Tyson, though he was far too considerate to say so. He'd obviously sensed that something was wrong, and was being very careful not to ask too many questions, although she knew he was bursting to know what had happened. She was so lucky to have him. Life without Jacob would be an empty life indeed.

When she saw Dylan across the road, she was so surprised she wasn't quick enough to react. She should have ducked into a shop, but she couldn't make herself move. He was locking the door of a dark blue van with the words 'D. Anderson, Electrician' on the side, and he looked up and caught sight of her. For a moment he simply stared at her, and she wondered if he was going to avoid her. Then he crossed the road, dodging between cars to get to her.

'Ellie.'

'Hello, Dylan.' Her voice sounded

strained, even to her own ears.

'How are you? How are Jacob and Baxter?'

'Fine. You?'

'I'm — I'm okay. I'm feeling pretty stupid, but other than that ...' He smiled at her.

'It's a shame you couldn't make it on Sunday,' she said, trying to keep her voice steady. 'Jacob was looking forward to it. I guess you were busy.'

He ran his hand through his hair, a sure sign he was stressed. 'Yes. Yes, I'm sorry I had to call off, but it was something that couldn't be avoided. I've had a lot on lately. Things will get better.'

She nodded, unsure of what to say next. 'Well, I'd better get going. I have to collect Jacob from school.'

'I'd offer you a lift, but I have an appointment. I'm already a few minutes late.'

'It doesn't matter. It's fine.'

'Is it?' He took her hands, his face suddenly serious. 'Ellie, I'm so sorry about all that Tyson stuff. I'm an idiot. I shouldn't have lied to you about her. You do know that I'd never deliberately hurt you? You believe that?'

'I —' She hesitated. The little voice urged her to reply that she did believe him; he wouldn't hurt her. But in spite of its urgent whisperings, she kept silent.

'I'm not Tom, Ellie. You have to know that.'

She swallowed. 'I know. Are you all right to meet up on Sunday? You can still bring Tyson, if you like. Or Mitzi, or whatever she's called. I'm sure Baxter is missing her.' She gave him a warm smile, but it soon died as he returned it with a stricken look. 'What is it?'

'I won't be able to come to the park for a while. I have things to sort out and I'm going to be busy. It's just for a little while, Ellie, honestly,' he protested as she pulled her hands away from his.

'I have to go.' She tried to walk away, no longer knowing what was happening or what the hell it was that he actually wanted, but he put his hands on her shoulders.

'I just —' He looked around, as if he was hoping to see the answer he was searching for written on a shop window or something. 'Will you trust me, Ellie? Please?'

Well, that was the million-dollar question. She thought about Tom, about all his lies, about everything she and Jacob had been through. Then she looked into Dylan's eyes and, in spite of herself, she nodded.

He pulled her to him and for one brief moment she allowed herself to be held, feeling the warmth of him enfolding her. She would trust the little voice, at least for now. She would believe that this man was telling her the truth. She had no real choice. She was in far too deep.

11

Wedding Day

Jacob looked so handsome in his suit that he reduced Ellie to tears. She adjusted his tie and pushed his fringe back a little, then kissed him. 'You look lovely. So grown up. I'm so proud of you,' she said.

Jacob looked embarrassed. 'I wish you could come with me, Mum. I won't know anybody there except Dad and Laura, and they'll be too busy kissing and stuff.'

'Your grandma will be there,' she reassured him. He didn't look too impressed by that. 'And maybe Auntie Clare will go, and your cousin Lewis.' Her voice faltered. She really wasn't selling this to him at all. He didn't like his father's relatives any more than she did, and he wasn't looking forward to the wedding. In fact, she thought, the only thing that had persuaded him to go was the promise of a buffet afterwards and the reassurance that he could help himself to as many sausage rolls and vol-au-vents as he wanted.

'Are your shoes all right? They're not pinching you?' She had told him over and over again to walk around the flat in them to get used to them, but he hadn't taken much notice. She pulled a box of plasters out of the kitchen drawer and took two of them out, slipping them in his jacket pocket. 'Just in case they start to rub. You don't want blisters, do you?' She smoothed down his hair for the umpteenth time then glanced at her watch. 'Your dad will be here in a minute. Are you all ready? Do you need the toilet?'

'No, I'm all right. What are you going to do this afternoon?' Jacob's face was anxious. 'Will you be okay?'

'I'll be fine,' she reassured him. 'I might start papering the kitchen, if I can be bothered. Or I might start that new book I've been meaning to read for ages. I'll have a nice peaceful afternoon. Don't you

155

worry about me. Promise?'

He nodded, but she saw he wasn't convinced. She turned away quickly, walking to the window to hide the tears that were suddenly welling up in her eyes. Honestly, she was getting so weepy lately. She really needed to pull herself together. But Jacob had been worrying about her since the sponsored walk. She had told him that she'd met up with Dylan and that he was too busy to meet them for a while, and he'd said nothing, but she knew he was confused about it. So not only was she upset about Dylan, but she was also upset about Jacob's feelings. Then there was the small matter of her ex-husband marrying the woman he'd left her for, not to mention the fact that they were expecting a baby together. And then there was this flat, which still looked rather dreary, no matter how many pictures, ornaments and pretty cushions she tried to cheer it up with. No wonder she was weepy, really.

'Your dad's here!' She turned away from the window, forcing a smile, and held out her hand. 'Come on, let's go downstairs. We don't want to make him late for his own wedding.'

Jacob hesitated, then took hold of her hand and reluctantly allowed himself to be led downstairs to the front door.

Tom was standing beside the car, all dressed up in a new suit, looking smarter than Ellie had seen him in a long time. He nodded at Jacob, then handed him a white carnation. 'Here you go. Buttonhole for you.'

Ellie pinned it to Jacob's lapel. 'There you are. You look marvellous — doesn't he, Tom?'

'What? Oh, yeah, yeah. Really grown up. Smart lad, aren't you?'

'Are you all right?' Ellie wondered why she was asking him the question. He was getting what he wanted, after all. It should be him enquiring how she was feeling.

'What? Oh, yes. Fine.'

He didn't look all right. He looked pretty glum, actually. No doubt he was feeling nervous. Public occasions had never been his strong point. Whenever they'd gone to parties or family weddings he'd always skulked in the corner, not wanting to make small talk or engage with people.

'Who's your best man?'

He looked uncomfortable. 'Haven't exactly got a best man. Two witnesses, Laura's brother and his wife. They're all we need really for a registry office.'

'Oh, right. Okay. Well, good luck with it all'

'Do you mean that, Ellie?' Tom asked. 'I know it must be really difficult for you. It's good of you to let Jacob come.'

She was quite surprised by this sudden change of attitude. Marriage must be mellowing him before he even got the ring on his finger. 'Of course. I hope you and Laura will be very happy.'

'Thanks. I appreciate that.'

He hesitated for a moment, as if he wanted to say something else, then seemed to think better of it. 'Come on, young man. Get in the car. We don't want to be late, do we? God help me, my life won't be worth living if I'm not there before she is.'

They got into the car and Tom drove slowly away. Jacob pressed his nose against the rear window, waving to Ellie until the car turned out of the road. She sighed and headed back into the flat. She needed to keep her mind off this wedding. There was no way she wanted to sit and brood, and she probably would if she let herself.

It didn't take long for her to realise, though, that it wasn't Tom or the wedding that was occupying her thoughts, but Dylan. She kept replaying their last meeting — his assurances that he wasn't Tom, his promises that things would get better. She thought about the moment during the sponsored walk when she'd been so sure he was going to kiss her. She felt a frisson of excitement as she remembered the expression in his eyes, and the way he'd moved so close to her she'd felt the brush of his skin against hers. She wished she knew what he was thinking, what was really going on. Was it his parents' bad marriage that was scaring him off?

Was that the problem? If so, could he overcome his fears and take a chance on her? She needed to do something to take her mind off it all. Maybe she would start to wallpaper the kitchen after all.

As she stood in the poky little room, surveying the bare walls that had taken hours to strip clear of bits of wood chip left by the previous tenant, she realised she didn't have the energy or the heart to tackle the chore today. She flicked on the kettle and took a mug from the cupboard. A cup of tea, a biscuit and a good book. That would help her while away a couple of hours.

Twenty minutes later, she'd drunk a mug of tea, eaten four biscuits and read the same page of the novel several times without taking in a word of it. It was no good; she had to get out of the flat. She would visit Angie. That was the best thing. She would take Baxter a treat and have a gossip with her cousin. Wayne would be at the football match. His team were playing away today, and he'd arranged to travel down to London with his pals and spend the whole day there. Angie would probably be glad to see her. Anything was better than staring at these four walls and brooding about Dylan and the romance that might never happen.

*　*　*

There was no answer when Ellie rang the front doorbell of Angie's house a short while later. She peered through the window, wondering if maybe Angie was in the kitchen listening to the radio. She had a habit of dancing and singing along to the latest tunes when she did her ironing. Though, of course, she could be out — perhaps doing a bit of shopping in town. Angie could never have enough tops.

There was no sign of anyone in the living room. The television set was switched off — proof that Wayne wasn't there, at least. Ellie stood, wondering what to do. She took out her mobile and rang Angie. If she was in town and alone, maybe she could meet her there. Ellie didn't have the money to buy new clothes, but she could stretch to her bus fares and a coffee in the Beehive.

As the mobile continued to ring, a thought struck Ellie and she peered through the letterbox. She could just about hear the dulcet tones of Olly Murs, Angie's major crush, whose latest song was set as her ring tone. So Angie was in, but where was she?

A faint bark came to her. Was that Baxter? He sounded too faint to be in the house. The garden! They must be in the garden. That was why Angie couldn't hear her knocking or ringing the bell. Ellie put her phone back in her bag and headed to the back gate. The house was terraced, and to reach the back way she had to pass a few more houses, then nip down the wide passageway that separated Angie's block of houses from the next. The passageway was wide enough for dustcarts and was mainly for residents to have access to their garages.

As soon as she turned into the passageway behind the gardens, Ellie's heart sank. She could hear raised voices and the occasional bark from Baxter as two women engaged in a vicious argument. She knew Angie's voice. What on earth was going on?

As she opened the back gate, she took one look at the scene and almost left again. Angie was in the middle of a bitter argument with Mrs Lancaster, who lived next door. Both women were trying to make their point in very loud and forceful tones, while at the same time attempting to gather up bits of clothing that were strewn on the path, and yelling at Baxter, who was chasing round and round the lawn with what looked like a pair of rather large Y-fronts hanging from his mouth.

'Baxter! Stop it, now!' Ellie made a grab for his collar and managed to pull him to a halt. He dropped the underpants and stood there panting and looking suspiciously as if he were laughing.

'Ellie, thank God. Baxter's really outdone himself this time,' Angie gasped. She handed Mrs Lancaster a pile of clothes and began to gather up the items that were lying on the path.

Mrs Lancaster glared at Ellie. 'You ought to be ashamed of yourself, leaving an untrained dog here while you swan off to a swanky new flat. If you didn't want to look after him, you should never have got him.'

'What?' Ellie looked in some bewilderment at Angie, who had the grace to blush and hang her head. 'What exactly has been going on here?'

'I'll tell you what's been going on here,' said Mrs Lancaster. 'That dog of yours jumped over the garden fence and had a great game pulling everything off my washing line. Knocked my prop over, snapped my line, trampled all my and Stan's clothes into the mud. And even that wasn't enough for the mutt.'

'Mrs Lancaster came round here to tell me what had happened,' said Angie, 'and Baxter followed her. He pulled everything out of her arms and so they've been trampled on for a second time.'

Ellie's mouth twitched and she bit her lip. It wasn't funny. She mustn't laugh.

But the sight of Baxter standing guard over a huge pair of underpants was quite amusing. Almost as amusing as the hammock-like bra draped over the water feature. Almost.

'I'm terribly sorry, Mrs Lancaster,' said Ellie. 'I'm sure it won't happen again. Perhaps we can wash and iron the clothes for you?'

'No we won't,' said Angie. 'Not after the insulting things she's just been saying about me and you. She can do her own washing.'

'You see? This is what I've had to contend with,' said Mrs Lancaster. 'Is it any wonder the dog behaves the way it does with someone like her in charge? You should never have left it behind. It's disgraceful. I've a good mind to call the RSPCA.'

'I don't think the RSPCA deals with abused underwear, Mrs Lancaster,' said Angie. 'Now,' she finished, as she retrieved the bra and Y-fronts and handed them rather gingerly, and with a distinct curl of the lip, back to her neighbour, 'you have everything back and there's no real damage. You can go home.'

'And what about my washing line?' demanded Mrs Lancaster.

'Quite right. I'll drop you a couple of quid through your letterbox later tonight.'

Mrs Lancaster glared at her. 'You need to make this fence higher. I want six-foot fencing along here before the week's out or I'll report you to the police and the council and —'

'Yes, yes, whatever.' Angie practically propelled her neighbour down the path and out of the gate. 'Call Ghostbusters for all I care. Just go.'

'I can't believe you were so rude to her,' said Ellie as they drank tea in the kitchen ten minutes later. Baxter lay quietly by her feet, obviously relieved to see her.

Angie nodded at him. 'That's the most settled he's been since you left. He's getting worse, he really is.'

'He shouldn't have taken the washing,' admitted Ellie, 'but you could have been more diplomatic about it.'

'Diplomatic? To her?' Angie banged her

166

cup on the table in disgust. 'I intended to be, of course I did, but you didn't hear the things she said. Stuff about me being a woman of loose morals, practically living with Wayne, and about how I was turning this place into some sort of refuge and she never knew who she was going to be living next door to next, and how I ought to make up my mind if I was running a hostel for the homeless or some sort of animal sanctuary. I mean, who does she think she is? It's my house! I'll have whoever I like here.'

'Yet you told her Baxter was my dog?'

Angie looked sheepish. 'I was just trying to disarm her, that's all. Said the first thing that came into my head. Honestly, what am I going to do with him? I hate to admit it, but the old bat's right. We're going to have to get six-foot fencing up, and that's more money and effort. Wayne's going to be thrilled.'

'What's it got to do with him?'

'Well, he'll be the one putting the fencing up. Besides —' Angie took another sip of tea and then shrugged. '— he's moving in with me.'

'No! I thought you said you didn't want him to!'

'I know. But then he didn't come round for a week and I really missed him. I mean, I really did. It's funny how you get used to someone and they come to mean so much to you without you even realising.'

Ellie said nothing, taking a sip of tea and trying to push thoughts of Dylan away. 'So what about Baxter? Is Wayne all right about him?'

Angie couldn't look at her. 'Wayne doesn't like him. Don't get me wrong, he'd never hurt him, but he did say he's on his last chance. I can't tell him about today's antics. I'm going to have to come up with some story about wanting a garden makeover and including new fencing as part of that, and just hope to goodness Mrs Lancaster doesn't come out while he's working and stick her oar in.' She reached over to Baxter and gave him a gentle pat. 'Hear that? You've got to be good from now on. You're in the

168

last-chance saloon, okay?'

Baxter snorted and Angie shook her head. 'Like he'll take any notice of that.' She looked at Ellie. 'What are you doing here today anyway? Where's Jacob? Oh!' She clapped her hand across her mouth in horror. 'It's today isn't it? The wedding? I'm so sorry, Ellie. I completely forgot. I'm such an idiot. How are you feeling?'

'I'm absolutely fine. The wedding doesn't bother me at all. You should have seen Jacob this morning in his suit. He looked absolutely adorable. Tom brought him a buttonhole, too. He's quite the handsome little man.'

'Who? Jacob or Tom?'

Ellie pulled a face. 'Definitely Jacob. I don't think of Tom as handsome anymore.'

'Too busy thinking about Dylan?' Angie watched her with a sympathetic expression on her face. 'Nothing to report there?'

'Nothing. I've not heard from him since that day in town. I guess I just have to be patient. He asked me to trust him and I'm trying to.'

'Wow! Real progress! You must be looking through the eyes of love.' She broke into a chorus of The Partridge Family song and Ellie nudged her. 'Shut up! I'm not in love.'

Angie switched to the 10CC song of that title and Ellie couldn't help laughing. Still, as she watched her cousin closing her eyes and swaying dramatically as she sang, she thought maybe the words to that song were quite appropriate. She was protesting far too much ...

12

The Blonde

The supermarket was heaving. Ellie barely had time to draw breath between customers, as queues stretched far back down the aisles.

'Bet you're ready for a cup of tea,' whispered Martha, her supervisor, as she replaced the till receipt for her halfway through the afternoon. 'See to this next customer and I'll put a notice up saying you're closing. Go and get a cuppa while you can.'

'Thanks, Martha.'

Ellie rushed off to the canteen and grabbed a cup of tea. She glanced at her watch. Just gone two. Another two hours and the store would be closing and she could go home. She stood up and headed back onto the shop floor, wondering if Angie would have given Jacob one of her

Sunday roasts for lunch, or if she'd need to cook something substantial for him when he got home. It was good of her to have him at such short notice. She wasn't supposed to be working today: they were usually really good about not calling her in on the Sundays Jacob wasn't with Tom, but it had been an emergency and Kylie had sounded quite desperate. Ellie would be glad to get home. She thought about the good old days when Sundays were a day of rest. Fat chance of that now.

Her checkout was at the far end of the shop and quite a walk. She dodged fully laden trollies, whining children and grumpy husbands, and ducked down the homewares aisle. She liked to look down there, imagining the things she could buy for the flat when she got the money to do so. There were some lovely summery things in stock at the moment, and she was desperate to add some homely touches to the place. The cream paint had improved the look of the living room substantially, but some new cushions would look lovely, and perhaps a rug?

Maybe a nice duck-egg blue? She paused for a moment, eyeing the throws and wondering how much she could spare out of her wage packet that month. Having calculated that it would probably just about stretch to four cushions and little else, she turned to continue her journey back to the checkout — and then stopped dead in her tracks.

Just ahead of her, examining the bedding, of all things, was Dylan. And he wasn't alone. Beside him, a young blonde woman in tight white jeans, a lilac T-shirt, and high heels was leaning over a half-full shopping trolley, issuing instructions as to which package she wanted him to pick up.

'That pink one there! The one with the patchwork effect. No, that's the double. Pass me the king size, silly.'

Dylan obliged and they stood, heads almost touching, scrutinising the duvet cover and pillowcases. There was a familiarity between them, an intimacy that was unmistakable. For one brief, glorious moment, it occurred to Ellie that maybe this was Kate, Dylan's sister-in-law, until she remembered Kate had hurt her foot. It had sounded like a really nasty injury, and she couldn't imagine she'd be shopping today, let alone in high heels. Surely, if Dylan had something to hide, he wouldn't have risked coming to Maister's, the very place where he knew Ellie worked? But then, Dylan knew she rarely worked weekends, and then only on the Sundays that Jacob was at Tom's. He wouldn't be expecting her to be here. He would assume he was safe.

Any lingering hope Ellie had had that there was a reasonable explanation for all this was crushed completely when she heard the woman say quite clearly, 'Well, I like it. I hate that beige thing we've got on our bed. The pink looks really pretty.'

She heard Dylan laugh. 'You've nagged me for months to change the colour scheme in that bedroom. Could you really see me sleeping in a pink bed? Oh well, your choice.'

Ellie didn't wait to hear any more. She was seized with panic that he would turn round and see her. She couldn't bear to think about it. She really didn't trust herself to stay calm if she came face to face with him — let alone this woman who was quite obviously the reason he had cancelled their meeting that Sunday, and was also, no doubt, the reason he was so evasive lately and had been avoiding her.

'I'm not Tom, Ellie,' he'd assured her. Well, maybe not, but he was just as bad. The little voice had been lying to her all along. She flew back up the aisle and cut through electrical goods instead, praying that they would choose another checkout to go to. She'd had enough lies and deceit to last her a lifetime. Whatever Dylan wanted from her, it was over. She had no intention of getting involved with someone like him ever again.

13

Baxter Goes Too Far

Ellie peered out of the bus window, seeing little through the pouring rain. It had been a long day at the supermarket, and she had a headache coming on. Being wedged against the side of the bus by a large gentleman with three bulging bags of shopping on his knee didn't help. She barely had a third of the seat to herself. The bus was packed and the buzz of voices seemed to be growing louder. Somewhere a mobile phone rang, and someone struck up a conversation with the person on the other end of the line, seeming not to care that everyone on the bus could hear every word they were saying. Why did people speak so loudly into their phones? she wondered. This woman was practically shouting. Didn't she mind that everyone was party to the information she was passing on about her recent doctor's appointment and what the urine sample had revealed? People were very strange.

Ellie tried to see where they were, but it was difficult to tell as the window was so streaked with dirt and rain. She couldn't see a thing through the front window because of people standing due to the lack of seats.

She tapped the large gentleman on the arm. 'Excuse me. Where are we?'

He shrugged. 'Not sure, love. Hang on. Edna!'

A tiny bird-like woman sitting a few seats down on the other side of the aisle turned her head. 'What?'

'Where are we?'

'Newton Street. Why?'

The man turned back to Ellie. 'Newton Street. Do you need to get off?'

Ellie nodded. 'I'm the next stop. Can I get by, please?'

The man huffed and puffed, trying to gather his three bags of shopping together. Hooking the handles round his fingers, he struggled to his feet and tried to stand back so she could get out of the seat. People were blocking the aisle and he knocked into someone who complained quite loudly. He apologized and tried again to move back. Ellie managed to squeeze through and stand in the aisle, but getting through the numerous passengers who were having to stand proved more difficult than she'd anticipated. She caught a glimpse of her flat as the bus went sailing by and tried desperately to reach for the bell.

'The bell! Can you ring the bell, please?'

A young woman standing by a buggy stared at her blankly. Her hand was cupped over the bell on the post. 'You what?'

'Can you ring the bell? I'm going to miss my stop. Oh, hell.'

Ellie made it to the front of the bus as it passed her stop. 'Can you pull over, please? I was supposed to get off there!'

'Sorry, love. Can't stop now. Not till the next official stop. You should have rung the bell,' said the driver helpfully.

Ellie gritted her teeth and clung on as the bus rattled down the road.

'Do you want this next stop?' enquired the driver eventually.

'You know I do.'

'Well, you haven't rung the bell,' he pointed out.

Ellie took a deep breath and rang the bell. The bus slowed and, thankfully, Ellie managed to squeeze past a group of four or five passengers who were trying to get on. Honestly, how many people was he going to let in? They were already packed like sardines in a tin.

She stepped onto the pavement and hitched up her bag, grateful to be on solid ground again, even if it did mean she had to walk back up the road in the pouring rain.

* * *

She'd almost finished papering the kitchen, and she was pretty certain that she could complete the job that evening before Jacob got home. It already looked so much better in there. She had managed to save up enough for a new blind for the kitchen window, and a lightshade that matched. It would look much more cheerful when it was done. If she hurried she could get the blind fixed and the lightshade up that evening, too. Then, she thought, it would be time to start on the bathroom. Now that really would be a difficult job.

'Ellie! Thank God. I thought you weren't coming back. I saw the bus go by and you didn't get off and I was worried —'

'Angie? What on earth's wrong?'

Angie looked awful. She was soaking wet and her face was lined with worry. 'It's Baxter. He's done the most awful thing he could possibly do. I really don't know what to do with him.'

'You'd better come in and tell me what's happened.' Ellie fumbled in her bag for her keys and began to unlock the front door,

'Hang on!' Angie ran down the steps

and splashed across the road to where her car was parked. Ellie watched in surprise as she opened the door and let Baxter out onto the wet pavement.

'Why have you brought Baxter? You know I'm not allowed dogs in the flat.'

'Please, Ellie. It'll only be for an hour or so. I couldn't leave him with Wayne. I dread to think what would've happened.'

Ellie sighed and stood aside to let them into the dark hallway. Baxter sniffed the air, not altogether approvingly. She couldn't really blame him. She'd never seen the downstairs tenants, but there was a horrible smell emanating from their flat. It was like soggy cabbage, dirty socks and mould all rolled into one. She had never heard the sound of a vacuum cleaner or a washing machine coming from there.

'Come on. Upstairs quickly,' she muttered, shutting the front door after her and hoping that Baxter wouldn't bark and alert anyone to his illegal presence.

The flat was even darker and drearier in this weather. The small windows didn't let much light in anyway, and on a day like today it was shrouded in gloom. Ellie did what she always did as soon as she got home in an effort to cheer the place up. She switched on the lamps in the living room and turned on the television, turning the sound down.

'Cup of tea?'

'Please.' Angie told Baxter to lie down and be a good dog, then followed Ellie through to the kitchen, looking around approvingly at the almost fully repapered walls. 'Wow! That looks much better. Makes quite a difference, doesn't it?'

Ellie filled the kettle and flicked the switch. 'I think so. It'll look even better when I get the blind and the new lightshade up. But never mind all that — what's going on with Baxter and Wayne?'

Angie nibbled her nail pensively. 'Well, you know Wayne moved in officially on Saturday?'

Ellie nodded.

'Yeah, well, he took this week off work so he could get settled in and do some odd jobs around the house. He's put the new fencing up, by the way,' she added. 'He couldn't see why we needed any till I showed him the broken panels and the leaning post.'

'You didn't have any broken panels and a leaning post,' said Ellie.

'Not at first, no. Took me absolutely ages to achieve that,' said Angie. 'Honestly, the things I do to keep the peace for that dog. And look how he repays me!'

'How does he repay you? You still haven't told me what happened.'

'What? Oh yes, well, Wayne was having a lie-in and I'd nipped to the shops. Thought I'd get some bacon and eggs and treat him to a full English breakfast. When I got back, all hell had broken loose. Baxter had managed to nudge open the door — my fault, I can't have shut it properly — and had gone upstairs and into our bedroom. Wayne was fast asleep and didn't hear a thing. Then he said he heard a kind of tearing noise in his sleep and it must have woken him up. When he sat up, Baxter was laying at the side of the bed, happily eating something. Wayne went to take it off him to see what it was and —'

'What? What was it?'

Angie raised her eyes to Ellie's and Ellie clapped her hand over her mouth. 'No! Tell me it wasn't —'

Angie nodded. 'It was. Wayne's scrapbook. Absolutely ruined. He'd been looking through it before he went to sleep last night — not for the first flipping time, it has to be said — and he'd put it on the floor next to the bed before he turned out the lamp. He's absolutely furious. Honestly, Ellie, when I got back I thought there would be murder. He kept yelling that it would have been a collector's item one day, and we could have passed it on to our kids.'

Ellie knew it was awful of Baxter and it must be a very upsetting situation for poor Wayne, but she still had to turn away to hide a smile. Honestly, she was so wicked. No wonder things never worked out for her. Karma was always at work, no doubt about it.

'I know you think it's funny,' said Angie.

Ellie turned back to her, ready to apologise, but saw the twinkle in her cousin's eye and couldn't wipe the smile from her face. 'I'm sorry. I know it must be horrible for you, and I know it was a very wicked thing for Baxter to do, but —'

'But the thought of Wayne's scrapbook being a collector's item is just too amusing for you to pretend otherwise,' finished Angie. She nodded. 'I know. I had to stop myself from laughing at first. Wayne shouting about how he'd planned to put it on eBay one day was too funny for words, especially when not ten minutes previously he'd been insisting it would have been a family heirloom. Thing is, Ellie, it's not that funny anymore. Wayne's absolutely sick of him. He says if I don't do something with Baxter he'll be moving out again.'

'He doesn't mean it. Things will calm down.'

'I'm not so sure they will,' said Angie. 'He's not a dog lover, and he's put up with a lot from Baxter lately. I don't suppose there's any chance that you could have him, is there?'

'Are you serious?' Ellie handed Angie a mug of tea and shook her head. 'You know I can't possibly have him here. There's a strict no-pets clause in the tenancy agreement. I think I'd be in trouble if the landlady knew he was here right now.'

'But he gets on with you and Jacob. He really misses you. His behaviour's just got worse and worse since you left.'

'Are you still taking him for walks? I know I haven't been taking him out as much lately, and I'm sorry for that, but I still manage two or three days. What about you? You're taking him out the other days, right?'

Angie looked guilty. 'It's not always that easy. I'm so busy, and he pulls so much. I can hardly control him. I can't always fit him in. But he's out in the garden a lot.'

'The garden's not big enough for him to have a really good run around and burn off that energy,' said Ellie. 'No wonder he's being so naughty. He must be bored stiff.'

'Ellie, please think about having him,' pleaded Angie. 'The landlady doesn't even live here. She need never know.'

'And suppose she found out? Suppose the tenants downstairs reported it? There's no way I could keep Baxter here without them hearing him. I can't risk being thrown out. Besides, look how small this place is. It would be impossible.'

'Well, can't you look for somewhere else? Somewhere bigger, that allows pets?' Ellie gave her a withering look. 'It took me eight months to find this place, remember? Do you think I'd have moved here if I'd been able to afford somewhere bigger? I'm sorry, Angie. Look, why don't you stay here for a couple of hours? Give Wayne time to calm down a bit. Then you can go home and try to smooth things over between him and Baxter. I'll start taking him for walks every day again, I promise. Tell Wayne that, and tell him that it'll burn off his excess energy and make him behave better. Just make him give him another chance.'

'And will you take Baxter for a walk

every day?'

'I will, I promise. I can't say whether it'll be morning or evening, because it depends on my shifts, but I'll fit a walk in every day somehow.'

Angie looked shamefaced. 'I'll try to take him out for extra walks, too, when I can. I should never have got him, should I?'

Ellie sighed. 'No, not really. You've never had a dog and you had no idea how much of a commitment they are. You really didn't think it through. But you were only trying to do a good, kind thing. Don't feel too bad about it, Angie. You've got a good heart.'

'Thanks. So, any news on the Dylan situation?'

Ellie didn't know how to tell her cousin what she'd learned. She felt such a fool for being taken in again. Hesitantly, she confessed about the awful discovery she'd made on Sunday. Angie listened, her mouth dropping open in shock.

'Never! I can't believe it. And he

sounded so nice. Just shows you. Are you absolutely sure she couldn't have been a relative? Or a friend, maybe?'

'There was something — I don't know — intimate about them. You know that familiarity that couples get? I got the feeling they'd pushed a supermarket trolley around together many times before. Besides, they were discussing *their* bedding, *their* bedroom colour scheme.'

'What a rat-bag. I'm so sorry, Ellie. I feel partly responsible. I should never have tried to persuade you to give him a chance. You should have listened to your famous little voice.'

'That's just it,' said Ellie. 'I did. Guess even my own little voice is lying to me now — and if I can't trust that, what can I trust?'

14

An Unexpected Visitor

Angie peered out of the living room window. 'The rain's stopped. I think I'll get off home now. Maybe Wayne's calmed down. Thanks for the drinks, Ellie.'

'Thanks for helping me finish the papering,' said Ellie with a smile. 'And thank you, Baxter, for being so quiet and not getting up to any mischief while we worked.'

'I know. Unbelievable, isn't it? You'd never think he could be so naughty at home.' Angie buttoned up her coat and then clipped Baxter's lead to his collar. 'Well, let's go and face Wayne. Hopefully he'll have calmed down. He may have rung round his old football mates, as I suggested. They may have some stuff they can give him. Maybe I can do him some photocopies, at least.'

They headed down the stairs and Ellie opened the front door.

'Thanks again, Ellie. I — oh!' Angie pulled a face and squeezed Ellie's arm. 'Looks like you've got a visitor.'

She turned away, leading a curious Baxter past Tom as he ran up the steps to the flat. Ellie heard him greet her cousin, but Angie only acknowledged him with a faint nod of the head. Baxter tried to investigate further, but she pulled him firmly away and across the road to the car. As she let him into the back seat, she peered across at Ellie and mouthed the words, *You okay?*

Ellie nodded and waved, then turned to Tom. 'I'm afraid Jacob's not in. He's gone for tea at Clare's.'

'I know. She mentioned. It's not Jacob I've come to see. I need to speak to you, Ellie.'

Ellie watched Angie drive away, then stood aside to let Tom in. What could he possibly want to speak to her about? Surely he wasn't cutting his access visits even further? But then if he was, he wouldn't bother to visit her to tell her. It would be a phone call, or more likely a text.

She led him upstairs and gestured to him to be seated while she headed into the kitchen and flicked the kettle on yet again. She looked round the kitchen and smiled. At least it looked more homely and a bit lighter. One thing achieved, at any rate.

Five minutes later she handed Tom a mug of tea and sat opposite him in the armchair. 'So, what can I do for you?'

Tom took a mouthful of tea and winced as the hot liquid scalded his throat. He put the mug on the coffee table and looked at her mournfully.

'Laura lost the baby.'

'Oh, Tom. I'm sorry to hear that.' She was, too. Nobody deserved to go through such pain. She knew how lucky she was to have Jacob. What would her life have been like without him? Poor Laura. 'Is Laura all right?'

'What? Oh yeah, yeah. She's made of strong stuff, you know. She's already talking about trying again.'

'Oh, right.' Ellie supposed everyone handled things in different ways. She wondered exactly why Tom had come to see her. All right, losing their baby was sad, but he had friends and family. Why tell her specifically? What did he want her to say?

'Thing is, I don't want to try again.'

Ellie took a sip of her drink. Surely he hadn't come round here to ask her advice about how to break it to Laura that he didn't want more children? It came as no surprise to her, knowing how he'd resisted all her pleas to add to their family. She would have been more surprised if he'd been enthusiastically planning more children. He was looking at her now, a strange expression on his face. What was wrong with him? Ellie shifted uncomfortably. He was making her uneasy. She wished he'd just go.

'Well, you'll just have to tell her, won't you? You need to discuss it with her. It's none of my business, Tom.'

'But I can't discuss it with her, that's

the thing.' Tom looked thoroughly miserable. 'She's not like you, Ellie. She doesn't listen. She just talks over me. Her and her mother. Christ, what a pair they are. I don't get a word in edgeways.'

Ellie hid a smile. *Welcome to my world*, she thought. So Laura was no pushover. Well, good for her. In spite of everything that had happened, Ellie was glad that the young woman had the strength to stand her ground. She was so young — not much older than Ellie had been when she married Tom. She could easily have submitted to his will the way she herself had. Ellie couldn't help but admire her.

'It's nothing to do with me, Tom. I don't understand why you're here. You should be talking to Laura.' She stood up, meaning to take her mug into the kitchen. She didn't feel like drinking more tea. She just wanted him to go and leave her alone.

He reached out and grabbed her wrist. 'I made a big mistake, Ellie. I know that now. When I look at you and Jacob, I see what I've lost. I don't know what happened, why I did what I did. There's only ever been you, Ellie, you know that. Laura was a massive error of judgement. I miss you. Give me another chance, please.'

Was he serious? The desperate expression in his eyes told her that he was. Ellie couldn't believe it.

'Your wife has just lost her baby, Tom. Your baby. Go home and take care of her,' she said.

'She'll be fine. Her mother's there. Her mother's always there. Look at me, Ellie. I'm still the man you fell in love with. Can't you see that?'

Ellie looked and could barely suppress a shudder. 'You're right, Tom. You are the man I fell in love with. You haven't changed a bit. That's why I know I wouldn't go back to you if you paid me a million pounds. You're still the same lying, cheating, selfish, weak man you always were. You've barely been married for five minutes. Your wife has just suffered a miscarriage, yet you're round here begging me to take you back, after everything that you've done. Look at this place! This is what you've reduced your son to living in because you were too busy spending our deposit money to impress your girlfriend. You didn't care what happened to him, you didn't care what happened to me. Now there's not a sign of grief for the baby you've lost or for the wife who's gone through such a dreadful experience. Why on earth would I want you back?'

'You make it sound so black and white,' Tom whined. 'It wasn't like that ...'

'I think it was exactly like that. Now can you go please? I have a blind to hang and a lightshade to put up before Jacob gets home.'

'I could help you while we talk?'

'I don't want to talk, and I don't want your help. Just go.'

Tom's eyes narrowed suspiciously. 'Is this about that Dylan bloke that Jacob keeps banging on about? Are you seeing him?'

Ellie flushed. 'No I'm not seeing him. But if I was it would be absolutely none of your business, would it? We're divorced, Tom. Now go home and take my advice. Try to sort things out with Laura and be honest, otherwise you'll have another divorce under your belt before the year's out, and two in one year is a bit much, even for someone like you.'

Tom gave her a look of disgust and got to his feet. 'You're absolutely right. I don't know what I was thinking, coming round here. I guess the miscarriage has messed with my mind. It must have done, to make me think I could ever be happy with you. I forgot for a moment how horrible it was living with you. Thank God you reminded me. I'm going home to my wife, and I'm going to take her the biggest bouquet of flowers that I can buy.'

'Good for you.'

Ellie shut the door behind him and heaved a sigh of relief. His final rant at her hadn't touched her at all. Nothing he said meant anything to her whatsoever. She smiled and hugged herself as she realised she was truly free of him. He couldn't touch her any longer. She should have listened to her instinct from the start. She'd known what sort of man he was from their first meeting, but she'd ignored that little voice warning her, because she'd wanted to believe in him. Well, she'd never ignore it again.

Then her smile faded and she sank onto the armchair, her mind whirling in confusion. That same little voice had trusted Dylan. From their very first conversation, it had whispered to her that here was a man she could believe in. What was going on?

'I'm not Tom, Ellie.' His words replayed in her mind over and over, and she knew he was right. He wasn't Tom. So what had happened? What was he playing at? She shook her head, impatient with herself. Whatever there was between them, it was over. As if to prove her point, she took out her mobile phone and, after a moment's hesitation, she deleted Dylan's number. It was a gesture of defiance. There was no going back now.

15

A Shocking Discovery

The park was crowded, even for a sunny August Saturday. Baxter and Jacob had had a fantastic time together, running races until Jacob's legs were too tired to run any further. Baxter, despite his panting, seemed capable of continuing indefinitely. In spite of his seemingly inexhaustible supply of energy, he sat patiently while Ellie and Jacob fed the ducks, then flopped at Ellie's feet as she sat on the nearest bench, watching her son play on the swings.

Ellie wondered if Baxter was missing Tyson as much as she was missing Dylan. In spite of the crowds of people milling around, the park felt empty to her without him beside her. She tried to ignore the loneliness that suddenly attacked her as she watched couples strolling hand in hand beside the lake. Was she destined to be alone for the rest of her life? Better that, she thought determinedly, than go back to Tom, or live with a liar for the rest of her life.

Try as she might, she couldn't think of a single plausible reason why Dylan would have been shopping for bedding with a glamorous blonde and discussing 'our bedroom' if she wasn't his live-in girlfriend. Or wife. Ellie sat up straight in shock as the thought occurred to her for the first time. What if all that stuff about marriage and children had been a lie, too? What if he was married and had made up all the stuff about divorce? What if he had kids? Oh, good grief. This was getting worse.

Baxter seemed to sense her unease and whined. She patted him and tried to calm herself down. Even if Dylan was a married man and a father, she had done nothing wrong. She hadn't even kissed him. That moment had been just that — a moment. It had passed. No harm done. She should be glad about that, not lying

200

in her bed night after night imagining how it would have felt to have his lips press against hers. It did no good to think about it. She had to get on with her life and forget all about him.

Jacob came and sat beside her. 'Can I have an ice cream, Mum?'

Ellie rummaged in her bag, blinking away tears as she remembered all the Sundays when Dylan would produce some coins and hand them to her son, ruffling his hair and telling him to get the biggest ice cream he could afford.

'Here. Get one for Baxter, too. I think he's a bit hot and bothered,' she said, handing Jacob some money. He ran off towards the ice cream van and she settled back in her seat and sighed. 'This is all because of you, you know that, don't you?' she told Baxter. He stood up, plonking his heavy head on her lap and looking up at her with sad brown eyes. 'If you hadn't come into our lives, I wouldn't have brought Jacob to the park that morning and we'd never have bumped into Dylan. And we literally did bump into him, didn't we? Well, you did anyway. Remember that, Baxter? Remember how you knocked poor Dylan flying? Do you miss him, too?'

She fondled his silky ears and he blinked. She thought it very likely that he did miss him. He'd absolutely adored him, there was no denying that. It seemed like all three of them had fallen under Dylan's spell.

Jacob returned and put the second ice cream on the ground for Baxter, who pounced on it eagerly. 'It's not the same without Dylan and Tyson, is it, Mum?'

Ellie swallowed. 'I — I suppose not.'

'Why did you fall out with him?'

'Who says I fell out with him?'

'You haven't seen him for ages. He never comes to the park with us anymore. I think Baxter's quite sad about that.'

'Is he? I expect he misses Tyson. I mean Mitzi.'

'I think you're quite sad about it, too.'

Ellie stared into her son's bright blue eyes. He looked back at her, his face solemn. How did one so young understand so much?

She squeezed his hand. 'It'll be all right, Jacob. I promise. Things will get better.'

She wondered who she was trying to convince — Jacob, or herself.

★　★　★

'Can I get *The Beano*?' They were passing the newsagent's on the way back to Angie's house. Ellie was dreading going back. The atmosphere in there had been awful when she'd collected Baxter that morning. Evidently things were still pretty bad between Wayne and Angie. Her cousin had had to do an awful lot of grovelling, and she had confided in Ellie that Wayne refused point blank to even acknowledge Baxter, who had been confined to the kitchen and garden when Wayne was in the house. Ellie thought it was no wonder Baxter looked so depressed. What a way to live.

'Go on then. I'll wait outside. Be quick.' She handed him some money and wound the lead round her wrist as Baxter tried to follow him into the shop. Mrs Wilson may have championed Baxter to Angie all those weeks ago, but Ellie doubted she'd welcome him into the shop.

She peered at the goods on display in the window. Jars of sweets, some plastic toys — the usual stuff you'd find in a newsagent's window. She patted Baxter as he pulled impatiently on his lead, and then wandered slowly past the door to the second window. There was a noticeboard behind the glass with several cards pinned to it. Ellie glanced at them, only half paying attention. A second-hand washing machine for sale. A young girl offering baby-sitting services. Baby rabbits for sale, five pounds each.

Ellie stood up straight, her stomach turning over as she stared at the card in front of her.

"Free to good home. Boxer dog, five years old. Good reason for parting."

The address was Angie's. Ellie couldn't take it in. What was Angie thinking? She couldn't possibly give Baxter away. He'd already lost one home; he couldn't lose another.

As soon as Jacob came out of the shop, clutching *The Beano*, Ellie grabbed his hand.

'What's the matter?' he asked, clearly surprised.

'Come on, Jacob. We have to hurry. I need to speak to Angie — fast.'

★　★　★

Angie looked over her shoulder and whispered, 'Wayne's in. It's not a good time to talk about this.'

'I don't care if it's a good time or not. What are you playing at? You can't just pass him on like some unwanted Christmas present. He's already been through this once before, remember?'

'Of course I remember. It was me who took him on, wasn't it? And I did try my best, Ellie, you know I did. I just can't make him behave himself, and Wayne really doesn't like dogs. It's him or Baxter, and what can I do?'

'You do know you're doing exactly the same thing that his previous owner did — choosing a partner over Baxter? The very thing that you were so disgusted about!'

'I know, I know. You don't have to tell me. I feel bad enough as it is. Do you honestly think I don't feel guilty about all this? I tried, Ellie, but there's nothing I can do about it. If only Baxter was better behaved, or a bit smaller. I can't force Wayne to like him; and if he's going to carry on eating scrapbooks, wrecking Wayne's jeans and dragging the washing from neighbours' lines, well, it's his own fault. I'm sorry, but that's the way it is.'

'I don't believe this.' Ellie looked pleadingly at Angie. 'Just think about it, please. Don't give him away to just anyone. He needs a proper, caring home. Please don't rush into anything.'

'I won't.' Angie looked uncomfortable. She took Baxter's lead from Ellie's hand and ushered the dog inside. 'Thanks for taking him to the park. See you tomorrow?'

Ellie said nothing. She was too sickened

to reply. She turned and guided Jacob down the path and out of the gate, not looking back at her cousin. She heard the front door shut and realised she'd been holding her breath. She let it out with a big sigh. Now what?

'What will happen to Baxter?' Jacob's face was pinched with anxiety, his eyes wide with fear. 'What if somebody cruel gets him?'

'That won't happen. Angie will check the new owner very carefully,' Ellie assured him. But would she? Or would she be so relieved to find a new home for him that she'd let him go to just anyone, the way his previous owner had?

'We've got to take him,' said Jacob. 'Please, Mum. He can live in our flat. He'll be good, I promise. He loves us. He'll behave.'

'I'm sorry, Jacob. I can't do that. You know I can't. We're not allowed pets in the flat. If the landlady found out she'd make us leave, and then where would we go?'

'She won't find out. She never comes

round.'

'But the other people who live in the house would hear him, and they might tell her.'

'He'd be quiet, I promise! He won't bark. He only barks if he gets upset or frightened, and he wouldn't be upset or frightened with us, would he?'

'Jacob, he'd go insane cooped up in that tiny flat —'

'We'd take him for walks all the time!'

'Not all the time. How could we? I'm at work, you're at school. He'd be so bored in there, and you know how destructive he gets when he's bored. Besides, we don't have the room for him.'

'He could sleep on my bed. I wouldn't mind. Please, Mum, please. Don't let them send him away to strangers.'

Jacob's eyes were bright with tears. Ellie gulped back tears of her own and squeezed his hand. 'I'm sorry, Jacob. I can't let him live with us. I wish I could, really I do. Angie will find him a good home, I'm sure of it. Please don't worry.'

Jacob wrenched his hand away from

her and marched in front of her, his head down. Ellie knew it would take a long time for him to get over this latest blow. If she had the power to put it right she would, but it was out of her hands. There was no one to turn to. Baxter's future was in real jeopardy, and there was nothing she could do about it.

16

Baxter Takes Control

Jacob wouldn't eat his breakfast and pushed away his beaker of juice untouched.

'You have to eat.' Ellie tried to keep the anxiety out of her voice. He'd barely spoken a word to her for the last two days, since her refusal to agree to taking Baxter on. He'd also hardly eaten a thing. She had no idea what she could do to make him understand that having a dog in this flat just wasn't an option, and finding alternative accommodation was out of the question for a long time.

'I'm not hungry.' He stood up and grabbed his school bag. 'Ready.'

Ellie put his dish and beaker on the draining board and picked up her bag and keys. 'Right. Come on then.'

They walked to school in silence. It

was so unlike Jacob to be quiet. Usually she couldn't halt his flow of chatter on the way to school. Occasionally she'd longed for him just to stop talking for a while. Now she wished with all her heart that he'd launch into one of his long discussions about something he'd read in *The Beano*, or which Thunderbird was the best, or what David had said in class yesterday that had made the teacher send him out to see the headmaster for the umpteenth time that term.

As they neared the school gates, Jacob suddenly turned to her. 'What if he's already gone?'

'I shouldn't think so. Angie never mentioned anything when we dropped him off last night after his walk, did she? I'm sure if she'd had a reply to the advertisement she would have told us.'

'She might not, in case we stopped him going.'

Ellie rubbed her forehead. 'We can't stop him going, Jacob. I'm sorry, but I've already explained this to you.'

'Will you go and check? Make sure he's

still there?'

'I have to go to work. You know I have to be there for ten. I'm working till six. That's why Auntie Clare's picking you up and taking you home for tea.'

Clare had proved a godsend. To Ellie's astonishment, Jacob and Lewis had really hit it off at the wedding, and Clare showed no signs of being anything like her brother, thank God. It was a shame, Ellie thought, that she hadn't got to know her better when she was married to Tom, but their mother had fallen out with Clare, and Tom always took his mother's side. It was a miracle that he'd overruled her and invited her to his wedding, and one that had paid off for Ellie as well as Jacob.

'After work? Before you come for me? Will you?'

Ellie hesitated, then nodded. It would mean a detour, and after eight hours at the supermarket she could have done without it. But if it would put Jacob's mind at rest, even temporarily, it would be worth it.

'Thank you.' Jacob's voice was small as

he shuffled through the school gates, his head hanging low. Ellie could have cried for him. She only hoped she really could put his mind at rest, and wouldn't have bad news to tell him that evening.

★ ★ ★

'You can't be serious.' Ellie felt the colour drain from her face as Angie broke the news to her.

'Tomorrow morning. They came to see him earlier and loved him. It's a good home, Ellie. He'll be happy there.'

'How do you know it's a good home? Have you inspected it?'

'Inspected it?' Angie rolled her eyes. 'I'm not the RSPCA. Look, they were a nice couple and they said they've always wanted a Boxer. They've read up on them and everything. I'm sure he'll be fine.'

'Read up on them? So they've no experience with Boxers? Have they got any experience with dogs at all? Have they owned a dog before? Do they understand the level of commitment needed?'

'Of course they do. They've read some books about it. They're taking it very seriously. They haven't had a dog before, no, but everyone's got to start somewhere. Everyone has to have a first dog, don't they?'

'But I don't think Baxter is the ideal first dog, do you?' Ellie searched Angie's face for some sign that Angie was having doubts.

'Look, Ellie, he's going tomorrow morning and that's that. I'm sorry but there's nothing I can do about it. Wayne already agreed with them and —'

'Wayne! I might have known. Did you actually see them? Did you talk to them?'

'Of course I did! Honestly, I'm not like Baxter's previous owner, you know.'

'Aren't you? I'd think about that one, Angie.'

Angie tutted. 'Okay, if you're going to be like that, you may as well go.'

She began to shut the front door but Ellie stuck her foot in the gap and prevented it from closing. 'Wait! Can I take him for one last walk? Please, Angie. Just to say goodbye?'

Angie opened the door again and folded her arms. 'Promise you're not going to do anything stupid?'

'Like what? There's nothing I can do! Don't you think if I had a choice I'd have taken him by now?'

'Hmm. I suppose so. Okay then. Wait there. Wayne's having his tea and it's probably best you don't come in at the moment.'

Ellie was quite relieved. She didn't trust herself to face Wayne, not feeling the way she did. She would be far too tempted to tell him what she thought of him, and her and Angie's relationship might never recover if she did.

'There you go.' Angie handed the lead to her, and Baxter leapt out of the front door onto the path, almost as if he couldn't wait to escape. 'See you later.'

She closed the door and Ellie followed Baxter, who was pulling hard on the lead, out of the gate.

She couldn't believe this was the last

time she would ever take him for a walk. How could Angie bear to let him go? All right, he had his naughty moments, but that was more from boredom than anything. He was a sweet, loving dog who just needed to feel loved and wanted. How could Wayne and Angie not see that? She felt tears pricking her eyes as she walked, wondering about the couple who were going to collect him the following morning. Would they be good to him? Would they understand him? Or would his excess energy, his low boredom threshold and his general bounciness infuriate them too before long, and lead to him being passed on to yet another home? What would become of him?

Jacob would never forgive her for this, she thought anxiously. If only Dylan were here, he would know what to do. She'd thought many times over the last couple of days that if only she'd got his address or kept his phone number, she could have contacted him about the situation. Even if the two of them weren't together and never would be, it didn't alter the fact that Dylan was very fond of Baxter, and Baxter obviously adored him. Dylan owned his own house and didn't have a dog already. He might have been per-suaded to take Baxter on. Why had she been so stubborn and so stupid that day and deleted his number, just to prove a point? She was an idiot. Now she had robbed Baxter of the one chance he might ever have of a good home. Really, how could things get any worse?

Baxter stopped suddenly and stood, sniffing the air. Ellie blinked and looked round. Where were they? Good grief, he'd led her to Glamis Avenue again. Oh God, he'd caught the scent of that cat, hadn't he? She made a lunge for his collar, but was too late. Baxter leapt forward with such speed that the lead was yanked from her grasp. She yelled for him as he bounded away from her, the lead trailing uselessly beside him.

She began to run, cursing her heels and the weight of her bag as she watched him streak along the pavement towards the pretty bungalow at the end of the block, where the cat that had tormented him so cruelly lived. She gulped as she saw him stand still, facing the gate. Her stomach churned as she heard him give a delighted bark, and then her legs almost gave way in fear as she saw him take a flying leap over the hedge into the garden.

'Oh, God, no! No!'

Fearing carnage, she picked up speed, her lungs straining as she charged towards the bungalow.

'Baxter, get here. Get here, now!'

She reached the bungalow and stood still, her hand clutching her side where she'd developed a stitch. Her breath came in gasps as she took in the scene in front of her. The pink mobile nail van had gone, and in its place was a dark blue van with the words 'D. Anderson, Electrician' in white script on the sides. There was no sign of any cat, but Baxter would probably not have noticed if there had been. He was too busy jumping up and down like an excited kangaroo, smothering a delighted Dylan with kisses.

'I — I don't understand.' Dylan? Was

he doing some work at this bungalow, then?

He looked up and saw her standing there, totally confused. 'Ellie. It's so good to see you. Both of you.'

'Are you — are you working here?' Ellie looked round, baffled.

Dylan gave her a gentle smile, and in spite of everything her stomach fluttered. 'No. This is where I live.'

'You live here?' Ellie gulped. She peered through the window, expecting to see the blonde woman appear at any moment. So it was Dylan's girlfriend who had the pink van. Dylan's girlfriend who had the arrogant cat. Well, when she'd thought things couldn't get worse, she'd been entirely wrong. Now she not only had the image of his girlfriend in her mind, but she could picture them together in this bungalow. And there was no way Dylan could take Baxter, after all. Not with that cat in the picture.

Dylan managed to prise Baxter off him and headed down the path, opening the gate for Ellie. 'Come in. Please. I'll make you a coffee.'

Ellie felt her insides turn to liquid. 'What about — I mean, are you alone?'

He looked surprised. 'Yes. Completely. Will you come in? Please? You and I have a lot to talk about.'

17

The Inner Voice

Ellie was trembling as she followed Dylan and Baxter into the bungalow. Baxter's tail was wagging so hard she thought he'd take off at any moment.

She was torn between wanting to be with Dylan, and the certain knowledge that she didn't want to see where he lived with his girlfriend, let alone come face to face with her. All right, she might be out at the moment, but what if she came back? How would Dylan explain Ellie's presence? Maybe he'd just tell the truth — that she was someone he'd met in the park and they'd sometimes walked the dogs together. That was all there was, after all. But why had he borrowed his sister-in-law's dog in the first place? That could be tricky to explain away. Ellie wondered if he already had a cover story planned.

He led her into a large, comfortable lounge and motioned to her to sit down. She perched on the sofa and then yelped as Baxter leapt up beside her.

'Baxter! Get down! I'm so sorry, Dylan, I don't know why he's done that. He never did it at Angie's.'

'It's fine, don't worry. I'll get you that coffee.'

He headed into what was presumably the kitchen, and Ellie sat, wondering what had happened and how she'd come to be in this position. Of all the coincidences! Baxter seeking out the cat that day, and all the time it had been Dylan's home. It was unbelievable, really. And for him to lead her to the same house again today — amazing. She frowned. Yes, it was amazing. And unbelievable. Something didn't make sense.

Dylan returned and handed her the coffee. She was surprised to see his hands were trembling. So he was nervous, too? Maybe he was worried his girlfriend or wife or whoever she was would come back early. She'd better drink this fast and get out of there; save them both an embarrassing scene.

'Oh Ellie, it's so good to see you. I can't tell you how glad I am to have you here, to be able to talk to you properly. I've been trying to pluck up the courage to call you all week, but I was so afraid you wouldn't want to know. It's fate.'

Ellie peered at him over the coffee cup. 'Is it? I'm not so sure about that.'

'You're still angry with me. I can't blame you, after all that stuff with Mitzi and then cancelling our meeting and not getting in touch for so long. Will you give me the chance to explain? To put things right?'

'I don't think so, Dylan. I don't think I want to hear any more of your lies.'

'My lies? You mean about Mitzi? Just one little white lie —'

'One little white lie?' Ellie put the cup on the coffee table and glared at him. 'You really think I don't know?'

He looked puzzled. 'Know what?'

'About a certain blonde lady who

223

drives a pink van. A lady who does nails for a living. A lady who owns a very fluffy and rather spoilt cat. A lady who doesn't like the beige bedding you have in your room but is rather keen on pink patchwork.'

He looked completely stunned. For a moment he simply gaped at her, then he ran his fingers through his hair and leaned back in the armchair, seemingly lost for words.

Ellie felt a moment's satisfaction and took another sip of her coffee. 'I'm good, aren't I? Who needs a clairvoyant with me around?'

Dylan shook his head. 'I don't understand. How could you possibly know all that?'

Ellie put her cup down and wrapped her arms around herself, trying to suppress the misery that suddenly engulfed her. He wasn't denying it. She should at least be grateful for that. Trying to keep her voice steady, she explained about Baxter's last visit to Glamis Avenue, his desperation to get at the cat who was so clearly tormenting him, and about the voice of the woman she'd heard calling for her "Cupcake". She then told him, not looking at him, about her unexpected shift at the supermarket, and how she'd heard him and the blonde discussing their bedding when she was standing only a few feet behind them.

'Oh God. What you must have gone through.' Dylan stared at her in horror. 'Oh, Ellie. I'm so, so sorry.'

'Don't be. It's over now and it doesn't matter.' She stood up and looked at Baxter. 'Come on, you. Time for home. Not that it will be home for you much longer.'

'Ellie, sit down. We have to talk about —' He stopped suddenly as her words sank in. 'What do you mean, it won't be home for him much longer?'

Ellie shrugged. 'Angie's decided she can't cope with him. She's giving him away to a couple who've never owned a Boxer dog before, or any dog come to that. God knows what will happen to him.'

And then the tears came. To her horror, she crumpled right in front of him, and dropped back down on the sofa, holding her head in her hands as she sobbed.

'Ellie, don't! Don't.' He was next to her in a flash, his arms around her, stroking her hair as she valiantly tried to pull herself together.

'I'm all right. Please don't touch me.' She didn't think she could bear it much longer. She'd wanted to feel his arms around her for so long, but now that it had happened she just wanted him to go away. If he continued to hold her she would give in, she knew it. The blonde would cease to matter. She would be lost.

'Do you really mean that?' His grey-green eyes were questioning, and she knew it was already too late.

'No.' It was only a whisper but it was enough. Suddenly he was kissing her, and she was kissing him back, and the little voice that should have been telling her to walk away now, while she still could, was strangely silent.

'We can't do this,' she murmured,

but he kissed her again, and she allowed herself to be pulled against him, a tremor passing through her as he cupped the back of her head and she melted into him.

Baxter suddenly leapt off the sofa and Ellie emerged from her trance. 'Oh God. Stop it — what are you doing?' She pulled away from him, trying to steady her breathing as he stroked her face softly. Dimly, she was aware that Baxter had trotted out of the living room and was heading into the kitchen. She really should stop him, but Dylan's eyes seemed to have locked her in their gaze. She couldn't move.

'Kissing you? Please don't stop me. I've been waiting to kiss you forever.'

'But what about your girlfriend? It's not right. You can't do this to her. You said you weren't Tom.' She had to be strong. His morals were evidently nonexistent.

'I'm not Tom. I'm nothing like him. You have to know that. You do know that, don't you?'

He pulled her towards him again and she yielded for a moment. There was no warning from the little voice. Evidently it was so disgusted with her it had packed up and moved out. She was lost for a moment in a world where she and Dylan were together forever, and there was no blonde, no cat, no pink nail van, no beige bedding ...

'What the —' She felt something land on her knee and stared down at the rather tatty, slightly chewed Father Christmas toy that Baxter had just dropped in her lap. She leapt to her feet in horror. 'You have kids?'

'What? No, no of course not! That's a dog toy.'

'Of course it is. Why would you have a dog toy when you own a cat?'

'I don't own a cat. Melissa owns a cat.'

'So why would you have a dog toy?' Nothing was making sense. If he did have kids, she was leaving right now. More than that, she was leaving town. She never wanted to see him again. She didn't care what the little voice had said. Or not said, as the case may be.

'Because I used to have a dog, and this

228

was all I had left of him. Oh, Ellie.' He ran his hands through his hair again and looked up at her, a sheepish expression on his face. 'Haven't you worked it out yet? Baxter was my dog. I'm the irresponsible owner.'

Of course he was. That was what had been nagging away at her ever since she'd seen him in the garden. Why would Baxter bring her to the same place twice? How could it be a coincidence that Dylan lived there? No wonder Baxter had been so delighted to see him that day at the park that he'd charged into him, knocking him over. No wonder he was so thrilled to meet up with him there every day. No wonder Dylan had said all that stuff about Baxter letting Tyson win a race. He hadn't been talking about dogs in general — he'd been talking about Baxter specifically. They already knew each other.

Melissa! He'd said Melissa had a cat. The blonde was the princess who wanted rid of Baxter.

'So not only are you an unfaithful boyfriend or husband or whatever, but you're also an uncaring dog owner, too. My God. Are there any more lies you'd like to confess to?'

'Okay, let's just get one thing straight. Yes, it was irresponsible and stupid of me to let Baxter go to just anyone. But I'm not uncaring. Far from it. And I'm not an unfaithful boyfriend. Nor am I an unfaithful husband. I'm not married. I've never been married. I told you that.'

'Then who is Melissa? And why didn't you tell me Baxter was your dog the very first time I saw you?'

He patted the sofa next to him and sighed. 'Sit down, Ellie. I promise I'll tell you everything.'

'Everything?'

'Everything.'

'From the beginning?'

He smiled. 'Promise.'

'Go on, then.'

'Well, I suppose it all began with the fire. I'd been going out with Melissa for a couple of years. It was nothing serious. Neither of us wanted to settle down, but we were having fun and it suited us both.

230

Then there was a fire at her place. She wasn't hurt, thank God, but she lost most of her stuff — and no, she wasn't insured.

'She needed somewhere to stay. So many people had been getting on at us, nagging at us that it was time we settled down. I'm thirty-two and Melissa is twenty-seven. They said we should be grown up and make some sort of a commitment.

'Melissa and I had already agreed that neither of us wanted children. I didn't trust myself to be a good father, and she's not the maternal type. She said her cat was the only baby she needed. That suited me, so finally I asked her if she wanted to move in with me.

'She had nowhere else to go and I suppose, like me, she was fed up with people nagging her to settle down, so she agreed. Her mother said she'd look after the cat, as there was no way she could stay here with Baxter around. Melissa had only been here a few weeks when she started to get this rash. It was all over her hands, and she was adamant that she'd only got it when she'd been stroking Baxter.

I didn't believe her at first. I told her to go to the doctor's. She did, and when she came back she said he'd confirmed that it was an allergy to dogs.'

'But one visit wouldn't have confirmed that,' said Ellie scornfully. 'She'd have needed tests to see what the problem was. Anyway, surely she'd met Baxter before if you'd been together for two years?'

'She had, but she informed me that the doctor had told her allergies can develop any time. She said we'd have to get rid of Baxter.'

'And you agreed? Just like that?'

'Of course not! I refused point blank. But her hands were so painful and raw, and she was getting in a real state about it. It wasn't going away, even though she was avoiding Baxter and washing her hands all the time in case she touched anywhere he'd been. It got to the point where she wouldn't let him in the lounge because she said his dog hairs on the carpet and sofa were causing a reaction. He'd always had free run of the bungalow, then suddenly all the doors were locked to him. He was pretty miserable.

'Then Melissa said she knew a couple who were looking to give a dog a home. She said they'd had plenty of experience, and that their dog had died a year previously but they were now ready to take on another one. I wasn't sure. She brought them round one evening, and they seemed genuine enough and really took to Baxter. I thought maybe it would be okay. I agreed to let them have him on a trial basis. If I couldn't bear it, or it didn't work out with them, Baxter would be returned to me.

'Melissa was delighted that I'd agreed, and kept promising me he'd be fine and I could still visit him whenever I wanted. He was supposed to be leaving at the weekend. I was dreading it, and spent all week psyching myself up for the big goodbye. Except I never got to say goodbye. I got home from work one evening and he'd gone. Melissa said that the new owners had just turned up, asking if they could take him that day as they were going on holiday and wanted to take him

233

with them so they could all get to know each other better. I was so shocked and upset that I never thought how ridiculous that sounded. I just —'

'You just what?' said Ellie gently.

He bit his lip and shrugged. 'I went to my room and shed a few tears. I admit it. It was all so bleak without him. I just wanted them to come home so I could see him. I started looking for him in all the old places I used to take him. Melissa was a lot happier, but it didn't take long for me to realise that her hands were no better. In fact, if anything, they were getting worse. Eventually she discovered that she was actually allergic to some of the stuff she uses at work, and Baxter had nothing to do with it. I said that meant we could get Baxter back, but she said she'd tried to contact the owners and they'd moved.

'I didn't believe her and we started arguing. A lot. To be honest, it wasn't working out living together, and I think we both knew it. But she had nowhere else to go, and neither of us seemed to have the nerve to put it into words.

'She'd been nagging at me for ages to take up running and get fit. I'd always resisted because I can't think of anything worse, frankly. Suddenly it occurred to me that it would be a great excuse to go to the park. I mean, it can look a bit dodgy these days, can't it? A single man in a park full of children, I mean. But no one thinks twice about joggers, and it'd be a great way to search for Baxter. If the new owners were still in town, they'd surely go to the park regularly.

'I'm not good at running. I'd never jogged in my life, to be honest. Fortunately, I'd only been twice when I struck lucky. I found Baxter — or rather, Baxter found me. I was so thrilled to see him, but really puzzled that he was with you. You definitely weren't one of the people who came to see him here. I was going to ask you what was going on, tell you who I was, but then you started ranting about the irresponsible owner who'd abandoned him to his fate, and telling me all about the card in the shop window and how nobody had even checked where he was going. I was completely baffled.

'I was far too embarrassed to admit who I was, but you asked me if I wanted to meet up with you again and walk our dogs together. It was a chance to see Baxter regularly, find out how he was, make sure he was being looked after. I figured that after a little while I'd come clean, once I'd persuaded you that I was a decent sort of person. Huh, really did well at that, didn't I?'

He gave an embarrassed laugh, but Ellie couldn't bring herself to respond. She'd thought he wanted to walk with them because he'd been attracted to her, when all the time it had been Baxter he'd wanted to see, not her. She felt so stupid.

'Anyway —' Dylan looked at her anxiously, but apparently felt it best to continue with his story. '— I came home, confronted Melissa, and discovered the truth.'

'Which was?'

'The couple who were supposed to be taking Baxter had backed out. The

236

husband had been offered a job, but it came complete with living quarters where no dogs were allowed. They'd explained it all to Melissa, but she hadn't bothered to tell me. Her excuse was that she was beside herself worrying about her allergy and just wanted to act while I'd agreed to Baxter leaving. She thought if I knew the couple had changed their minds, I'd change my mind too. She was quite right; I would have. It was all too late by then, of course. And it was the final straw for me and Melissa. She'd moved that damn cat in, and between them they were driving me insane. I didn't know how much more of them I could stand, but I was trying so hard to be responsible and grown up, the way everyone wanted me to be. But, then, there was you, Ellie.'

He took hold of her hand. 'You were so easy to talk to, so good to be around. I found I was looking forward to visiting the park as much to see you as Baxter. Soon I realised I'd still want to see you, even if Baxter wasn't there. That said a lot to me, and it scared me.'

'Scared you? Why?'

'I'd never wanted to get that close to anyone. I'd seen what a vicious divorce could do. I thought marriage inevitably ended in anger and pain and bitterness. I didn't want to go anywhere near it. Then I met you, and I saw the way you coped with Tom's betrayal, and the way you kept things so civilised for Jacob's sake, and I began to wonder if maybe things could be different. I loved being around Jacob. I could see myself having children of my own for the first time in my life.

'That day on the sponsored walk, walking with you and Jacob and Lucy ... I let myself fantasise for just a moment that you were my little family. It felt so good. I didn't know what had happened. I only knew I wanted to be with you. You took the fear away. And that's when I knew I had to back off, fast.'

'But why? If you thought that, if you wanted me ... You almost kissed me that day, and then you just pretended nothing had happened. Do you know how much that hurt me?'

'How could I do anything else? You'd been through so much with Tom and Laura. There was no way I was going to behave in the same way. I had Melissa to think of, too. We weren't madly in love, but she was still living with me and she deserved the truth. So I sat her down and explained it all to her.'

'Explained what?'

'Everything. The day after the sponsored walk, I told her I'd met someone who I thought I had a real future with. That's why I couldn't meet you that morning. I knew I had to be honest with Melissa. I told her that nothing had happened between us yet, but that I really wanted it to. I told her that, although I could hardly believe it myself, I could see the time coming when I wanted everything I'd run away from for so long — marriage, even children. And I told her that it was all because of you and how I felt about you.'

'But you'd never mentioned her to me all the time we were meeting up at the park.'

'You told me Angie had been here; that she'd met Melissa. I was worried that if I told you I was living with someone, things would get complicated — that I'd trip up somehow, mention her name or something, and you'd find out I was Baxter's owner. It was safer to not mention her at all. It wasn't that I was trying to deceive you because I was planning some sort of affair or anything. I wasn't. At first, I admit it was all about Baxter. Then I just wanted to spend time with you. As a friend, I mean. I wasn't expecting to develop these feelings for you, or I'd have been honest from the start. With you and Melissa.'

Ellie hesitated, but the little voice was still silent. She squeezed his hand. 'So how did she take it?'

'She was okay about it, actually. She was more worried about where she would live, but I told her there was no rush and I'd help her find somewhere. And I did. We found a nice flat for her and Cupcake, and I lent her the deposit money. I even took her shopping to replace the stuff she'd lost in the fire.'

'Like bedding?'

He grinned at her. 'Like bedding. I'm so sorry you had to go through that. If I'd known you'd seen us, I would have explained everything straight away.'

'Why didn't you tell me? After the sponsored walk, at least.'

'I just wanted — needed — to get things sorted out properly before I told you how I felt. I didn't want you caught up in any mess. I knew you were suspicious of men after what Tom did, and I wanted everything to be up front from the start. I was afraid you wouldn't want to get involved with someone who had such a lot to sort out. I needed to wait till Melissa moved out before I told you how I felt. I was trying to be fair to you, so we'd have a clean page to start afresh, and I also wanted to be fair to her. I didn't think it was right to start a proper relationship when she was still living here. Do you see that?'

Ellie could barely speak for the tears that were threatening to choke her. She nodded silently, and he peered at her closely. Then, seeing the tears spilling over her lashes, he took her in his arms again and held her tightly.

'It's been agony waiting for Melissa to move out. I was so afraid you'd move on and forget me.'

'Forget you?' Ellie laughed through her tears. 'I could never forget you. I can't think of anyone but you.'

He cupped her face, his eyes shining. 'I love you, Ellie. I would never want to hurt you, and I'll do everything I can to make you happy if you'll let me. Will you let me?'

She gulped and nodded, and he wiped her tears and kissed her lips. The little voice in Ellie's head finally spoke up and whispered, *I told you so!*

* * *

'So which room do you reckon, Jacob?' Dylan nodded at the two open doors and smiled at the little boy as he ran between them, Baxter following closely behind him. Jacob checked out the view from each window while considering the matter carefully.

'I think this one. It overlooks the garden and I'll be able to keep an eye on Baxter, even when I'm doing my homework,' said Jacob eventually.

'This one it is, then. We'll have a trip to the DIY shop this afternoon, shall we? You can pick out some wallpaper. I wonder if they do a *Thunderbirds* design?'

'Really? Brilliant!' Jacob threw his arms around Baxter's neck and hugged him. 'Not long now, Baxter. We'll be moving in next Saturday, straight after the wedding. Then you won't ever have to miss us again.'

'You really know how to make him happy,' said Ellie. '*Thunderbirds* wallpaper? He'll love you forever.'

'And while we're there, you and I can get some ideas to completely redecorate this place to your taste. And we'll start by buying new bedding,' murmured Dylan, putting his arms around Ellie and smiling.

'Definitely not beige.'

'Most definitely not. I'll even let you get pink, if you like. Or shall we save that for the nursery?'

'The nursery!' She laughed and nudged him. 'You're getting a bit ahead of yourself, aren't you? What happened to the man who never wanted marriage, never wanted children?'

'He's long gone,' said Dylan, nuzzling her neck and giving a contented sigh. 'And it's all because of you.'

'Oh no it's not, Dylan,' called Jacob, laughing as the Boxer chased him out of his new bedroom and along the hallway, barking joyfully. 'It's all because of Baxter!'

We do hope that you have enjoyed reading this large print book.

Did you know that all of our titles are available for purchase?

We publish a wide range of high quality large print books including:
Romances, Mysteries, Classics
General Fiction
Non Fiction and Westerns

Special interest titles available in large print are:
The Little Oxford Dictionary
Music Book, Song Book
Hymn Book, Service Book

Also available from us courtesy of Oxford University Press:
Young Readers' Dictionary
(large print edition)
Young Readers' Thesaurus
(large print edition)

For further information or a free brochure, please contact us at:
Ulverscroft Large Print Books Ltd.,
The Green, Bradgate Road, Anstey,
Leicester, LE7 7FU, England.
Tel: (00 44) **0116 236 4325**
Fax: (00 44) **0116 234 0205**

AN UNEXPECTED LOVE

Angela Britnell

Kieran O'Neill, a Nashville songwriter, is in Cornwall, sorting through his late Great-Uncle Peter's house. Since being betrayed by Helen, his former girlfriend and cowriter, falling in love has been the last thing on his mind . . . Sandi Thomas, a struggling single mother, has put aside her own artistic dreams — and any chance of a personal life — to concentrate on raising her son, Pip. But as feelings begin to grow between Kieran and Sandi, might they finally become the family they've both been searching for?

PALACE OF DECEPTION

Helena Fairfax

When a Mediterranean princess disappears with just weeks to go before her investiture, Lizzie Smith takes on the acting role of her life — she is to impersonate Princess Charlotte so that the ceremony can go ahead. As Lizzie immerses herself in preparation, her only confidante is Léon, her quiet bodyguard. In the glamorous setting of the Palace of Montverrier, Lizzie begins to fall for Léon. But what secrets is he keeping from her? And who can she really trust?

SHADOWS AT BOWERLY HALL

Carol MacLean

Forced to work as a governess after the death of her father, Amelia Thorne travels north to Yorkshire and the isolated Bowerly Hall. Charles, Viscount Bowerly, is a darkly brooding employer, and Amelia is soon convinced that the stately home hold secrets and danger in its shadows. Then a spate of burglaries in the county raises tensions amongst the villagers and servants, and Amelia finds herself on the hunt for the culprit. Can Charles be trusted?

SUMMER'S DREAM

Jean M. Long

Talented designer Juliet Croft is devastated when the company she works for closes. She takes a temporary job at the Linden Manor Hotel, but soon hears rumours that the business is in financial difficulties — and suspects that Sheldon's, a rival company, is involved. During her work, she renews her friendship with Scott, a former colleague. At the same time, she must cope with her growing feelings for Martin Glover, the hotel manager. Trouble is, he's already taken . . .